GLAD
to be

Left
Behind

GLAD
to be

Left
Behind

—— Dudley Hall ——

Treasure House

An Imprint of

Destiny Image® Publishers, Inc.

P.O. Box 310

Shippensburg, PA 17257-0310

"For where your treasure is, there will your heart be also."
Matthew 6:21

ISBN 0-7684-2961-7

For Worldwide Distribution
Printed in the U.S.A.

1 2 3 4 5 6 7 8 9 10 / 09 08 07 06 05 04

This book and all other Destiny Image, Revival Press, MercyPlace, Fresh Bread, Destiny Image Fiction, and Treasure House books are available at Christian bookstores and distributors worldwide.

For a U.S. bookstore nearest you, call
1-800-722-6774.

For more information on foreign distributors, call
717-532-3040.

Or reach us on the Internet:
www.destinyimage.com

Dedicated to Scott Deere

A life that ended too soon.

Scott, I miss you. I must apologize for not paying enough attention. I apologize also for my part in a world that didn't offer enough hope. I feel sure that you concluded somewhere along the journey that you would never measure up. You saw your dad and his friends as valuable, but you didn't feel that way about yourself. I wish you could have known—you are as vital to God's story of redemption as Abraham, Moses, Paul, and Peter. We didn't tell you in ways you could understand.

You know what, Scott? God trumped you. You did play a big role. You have affected me. I am more inclined to fight because of you; fight for hope. I don't want to stand by the graveside of any more young men or women who died not knowing their part in God's drama. I know you would encourage me to live "outside the box"...confront...correct. You were an outside-the-box guy yourself.

I know I don't have all the answers, Scott. But I know we can't keep promoting hopelessness and offering meaningless answers to people who need mercy and meaning. I hope I can help some. Thanks for your help.

Your friend,
Dudley

Acknowledgments

I owe a great debt to so many who have encouraged this writing. The hungry eager faces of young and old, who perplexed by the seeming negativism proclaimed even from pulpits, have begged for some real answers. I could not forget those faces as I would read again from the pages of Scripture. With renewed vigor I too wanted to know what hope is available for us now. I too was tired of worn-out prophecies telling of upcoming fulfillments of Bible verses taken too lightly. I am glad someone asked and helped me reexamine my own views adopted more by default than diligent study.

Of course my family had to bear the burden of a man with a book inside. I don't know if being with child is like being "with book", but one can act as strange as a pregnant woman when the gestation is under way. My son, David, took the lead especially in the last stage when I spent time in the hospital and recovery. Without his help we would never have gotten to press. My daughter, Karis, was always the encourager as she would read the manuscript with delight and ask questions that really helped. My wife, Betsy, as usual did double duty as she nurtured me to health while making valid suggestions and working to get the manuscript ready on time.

My dear friend, Glenda Williams, donated hours of talented time rewriting and adding some "feeling" to the narrative. She was so supportive and a wonderful partner in the whole project.

She is a real author and I hope one day soon she will be recognized for the gifted person she is. Until then she is delightfully content to teach others.

Wade Trimmer has been a great source of support as well as Alan Wright. These two pastors are working with people who need hope for living, and I trust their advice. Russell Thornberry who read the first notes was a constant support and reminder that the people he was trying to help needed a fresh look at hope and meaning.

Kay Moreno, an accomplished editor and leader of women, gave lots of encouragement to deal with the "important issues", as she would say. Thanks to Jimmy James, a lifelong friend, who worked to find the right mix of publisher and writer. And there is a group of friends called the Circle of Servants who surround our ministry with their love and prayers. They have been patient and life-giving to me. I hope the book helps each of them in their own ministries.

It was so refreshing to find within the publishing industry men like Don Nori and Don Milam who want to get a message of hope on the shelf. I have been blessed by touching their vision.

Finally, I am grateful for those who are willing to have open, honest discussion about controversial topics. I have been challenged by secure people who without rancor have presented different views and their reasons for them. For all who have wished for another voice in the midst of too much confusion, thanks for reading.

Endorsements

Glad to Be Left Behind is a courageous book. It challenges Christians to reexamine much of what passes for "truth" against what the Scripture actually teaches. Dudley's insight and easy reading style is, as usual, a breath of fresh air as well.

Dennis Peacocke
Strategic Christian Services
Santa Rosa, California

Glad to Be Left Behind, by my friend Dudley Hall, is simply written, reader-friendly, biblically sound, logically convincing, and hope-begetting. In these days of "gloom and doom," rapture-fever escapism, this book will stir up biblical hope, refocus your vision from defeat to victory, and prompt you to be a more passionate worshipper, a more powerful warrior, and a more productive worker.

Pastor Wade Trimmer
Grace Fellowship of Augusta
Augusta, Georgia

For those whose worldview has yielded less than triumphant hope, for those whose eschatology has robbed them of excitement and expectation and has left only a hope for a "quick escape" in their place, and for those who have secretly longed to have a perspective that produces constant and dynamic incentive to overcome until He comes...*Glad to Be Left Behind* is an absolutely must read! Couched in a readable dialogue style, this work avoids arrogant claims and accusative attacks and invites us to a "let's talk about this" meeting.

Jack Taylor
President, Dimensions Ministry
Former Vice President, Southern Baptist Convention

Glad to Be Left Behind is a book capable of equipping a generation of difference makers in a sea of escape takers. With great clarity and ease of understanding Dudley employs the powerful use of a story to transform an anemic paradigm that has left the Church behind in the discipling of the nations. This book carries the power to raise up a multitude of "Uncle

Herm's" who embrace a theology of occupation rather than that worn-out mind-set of retreat.

Pastor Norm Willis
Christ Church Kirkland
Kirkland, Washington

Would to God that every believer caught up in this present last-days craze could sit on Uncle Herm's porch and be taught the "big story" with emphasis on God's plan, above denominational distinctives and eschatological mumbo jumbo. This book provides a refreshing exaltation of the ultimate Israelite, Jesus Christ. After reading it, I'm glad (like Noah and Lot) that I was left behind.

Pastor Arthur "AJ" Johnson
Doers of the Word
Birmingham, Alabama

Dudley Hall in his excellent book, *Glad to Be Left Behind*, superbly shows us why the Church has become weak, passive, ineffective, and irrelevant in today's world. The pseudo-teachers of endtimes have told us our only hope is to escape from this life, leaving us for now, in defeat and despair. Dudley recaptures our focus from leaving earth to changing our world. It's a message of hope and victory *now*! I highly recommend this book to any serious Christian.

Pastor Rick Godwin
Eagle's Nest Christian Fellowship
San Antonio, Texas

Dudley Hall seeks to transform what many of us believe to be "popular error" that, for whatever reason, seems to be forcing itself upon the larger Body of Christ. You would have to slice bread quite thin, for it not to have two sides. This, in my opinion, is a careful and passionate presentation of "that other side" of future events that urgently needs to be known and embraced. The section entitled "Honoring Israel and Exalting Jesus" is worth the price of the book. Read it.

Bob Mumford
Lifechangers
Cookeville, Tennessee

Glad to Be Left Behind introduces complex theological ideas in a user-friendly way. I also think that it will help people understand what the Christian life is all about without being unduly negative towards those of a different persuasion. The approach is positive and reasonable—unusual in eschatology.

Dr. Gerald Bray
Beeson Divinity School, Samford University
Birmingham, Alabama

Table of Contents

Foreword

"Many years ago there was an emperor who was so fond of new clothes that he spent all his money on them. He did not give himself any concern about his army; he cared nothing about the theater or for driving about in the woods, except for the sake of showing himself off in new clothes."[1]

All was lovely in the emperor's kingdom until two conniving con artists appeared in the royal court purporting to be weavers extraordinaire and claiming that they had discovered a material so exquisite that only the elite could appreciate it. In fact, the rascals claimed, their designer clothes were so stunning that they had the unique quality of being invisible to those unfit for leadership or not intelligent enough to appreciate them.

The gullible emperor was allured by the thought of having such special clothes and, he thought, how nice it would be to distinguish the intelligent from the fools in his land. So he hired the phony weavers at a costly price. Wanting to know how the foreign designers were progressing, the emperor decided to send in his prime minister for an advanced glimpse of the garments. Surely, the faithful, old prime minister would be intelligent enough to see and appreciate the weavers' handiwork. When the noble statesman went in to behold the rogues working at empty looms, he found himself in a dire predicament. He was an honest

13

man, but to say that he just couldn't see the clothes would be to admit his own stupidity. He stared and stared—then, swallowing hard, announced to the phony designers, "Oh, it is most elegant, most beautiful!...What a fine pattern...I will certainly tell the emperor how pleased I am...."

He bluffed his ignorance and rambled on to the emperor about how exquisite the stuff was.

When the emperor got his first "viewing" of his new parade suit, he, of course, saw nothing, but was flanked by his best officials urging him to appreciate the intricacy and beauty of the suit. On the day of the great procession, the con men pretended to adorn the emperor garment by garment, and the emperor donned his new clothes for all the citizens to see. Word had spread throughout the kingdom that only the smart and sophisticated could see the new clothes, so, as the naked emperor marched down the byways, the onlookers pretended to be impressed, calling out "How beautiful! Oh look at the train of his robe!" The proud emperor was delighted. None of his previously paraded outfits had ever drawn such raves. All was well until...

A little child hollered out, "He has nothing on!"

The spectators, given courage by the innocent child, one by one began calling out likewise, "The Emperor has nothing on!"

Dudley Hall has stood in the crowd, watched the procession for years and now, with humble, honest eyes has dared to call out, "The emperor has no clothes!"

I started following Jesus as a fourth grader in 1972. Over the years, I went to great churches with great preachers, joined numerous Bible studies, was committed to several small groups, had mountaintop experiences on weekend retreats, graduated college Phi Beta Kappa with honors in Religious Studies, finished seminary as valedictorian, studied Greek, preached the gospel almost every Sunday for the last 15 years and have written three books. But I have had almost zero confidence to say anything to anybody about the endtimes. Every time I have poked my head into the weavers' workroom to see what the eschatology experts are spinning, I haven't been able to see it and have figured, "It must be me. I'm just not advanced enough." Others have stood beside me and said, "Isn't it marvelous? Isn't it intricate? Isn't it amazing how it all ties together and fits the times?" Sadly, like the insecure prime minister, I have mumbled my approval of what I couldn't see. I have, at best, stayed silent about what I couldn't see, but never dared to look much deeper because, after all, who was I compared to the master weavers who had gone before me and of whom all my colleagues praised?

I did preach one sermon series on the Book of Revelation about 10 years ago, but danced and dodged about well enough to never admit that I couldn't see the emperor's clothes. Partly, I've been lazy. I just didn't want to spend the time with all those prophetic charts; it made me feel like I was back in Algebra again. Partly, I've rationalized, "It's just not my thing; I'm a pan-millennialist—it'll all just pan out in the end."

Then, two years ago, I was compelled by the Holy Spirit to preach a series of messages on the Kingdom of God. A year and a half later, I found myself still preaching the same series. And, still, I can now hardly open my mouth from pulpit or pillow without talking about the Kingdom of God. Nothing has built my faith more, nothing has propelled me to believe for the miraculous more, than my consuming obsession with the Kingdom of God.

As I studied the pertinent New Testament passages of the Kingdom, I became absolutely certain of at least two things: 1) This Kingdom has already come; 2) My life must be devoted to conquering more territory for this Kingdom's King.

Through all my puny attempts to understand the charts and prophetic timelines, I had basically surmised this conclusion: The world gets worse and worse; the enemy gets stronger and bolder;

15

we seek to remain faithful so we can escape in the rapture; and then, somebody gets to be a part of a great, victorious millennium in the future. You can imagine the mental collision that took place as I tried to reconcile the seeming beauty and intricacy of the prophetic projections of world doom with my simple, triumphant New Covenant proclamation that the Kingdom is in our midst.

So, thank you, Dudley Hall, for saying what you see. As you speak about the profound hope we have because of Jesus' inauguration of a New Covenant and an "already" Kingdom, I think I finally have the courage to speak up too.

In his classic, "The Emperor's New Clothes," Hans Christian Andersen's finger is not pointed at the evil of the conniving weavers, but at the cost to the thoughtless crowd. Likewise, you will not see Dudley Hall's finger pointed in these pages at the "weavers" of pre-millenial dispensationalism. There are, of course, charlatans in every trade, including my appointed field of Bible exposition. But, those who use the Bible purely for gain are few. The preachers of different end-times messages are well-meaning. This isn't a book meant to critique other eschatological teachers. This is a book meant to open the eyes of the onlookers like me. This book isn't an exercise in theological sparring. It is an urgent, clarion call to Christians to awaken to the strength that we already have—our victory is nigh. Together, we can change the world! Wouldn't our enemy delight in us postponing our Kingdom-advancing efforts to the "sweet by-and-by"?

Yesterday, an accomplished surgeon in my church told me of his frustration with a Christian patient who refused to receive treatment for her cancerous breast tissue because she said that Jesus would come soon.

I say, let there be treatment not only for that dear lady's breast cancer, but let us treat all the cancers of the world—the rebellious growth of consumerism, the metastasized me-ism, the malignant depression. I have hope not only that we will enjoy

16

Heaven someday, but I have hope that we can bring Christ's healing message to every corner of the world today. And so does Dudley Hall. And, oh, what hope he has. May your heart be filled with that hope too, beloved reader, so you will see what is truly magnificent, beautiful, and intricate in the design of God's destiny for the world that is woven through the pages of His Word.

Alan D. Wright
Senior Pastor, Reynolda Presbyterian Church
Winston-Salem, NC

---

[1] Hans Christian Andersen, "The Emperor's New Clothes," in *The Book of Virtues*, William Bennett, Simon and Schuster, New York, 1993, p. 630.

CHAPTER 1

The Armageddon Discussion

It had been a hard day. The funeral had been filled with an atmosphere of despair. They all had been there, but no one was quite sure what to think. He had not exactly been a close friend, but he had certainly been more than an acquaintance.

It was a tragic car wreck...but this one had been intentional. It was clear—he had meant to do it. Only 19, he had seemed pretty down for the past several months, but no one thought much about it. He had lost his job, and his girlfriend had dumped him. But he was still going to church, so his friends weren't really worried about him.

He had become a Christian at youth camp five years earlier. When he got saved, he really got saved. He had been so excited. Just knowing that he was forgiven and that God loved him even if no one else did thrilled him. The thought of going to Heaven was reassuring, while the belief that life would now be better because of his newfound religion filled him with hope. But far from solving everything, his life just got more complicated. Girls, cars, friends, jobs, drugs—everything demanded a decision. It was more than he could handle.

School was not any better. In fact, he got depressed just thinking about it. His education left him feeling like a product of chance—an elemental accident. "There's no absolute right or wrong," he was told. "You have to figure out what works for you." But what kind of purpose and meaning could be found in

19

a random life with no standards? Sure, his teachers and coaches encouraged him to do his best, but what was the point if it didn't mean anything?

His family life was boring as well. His mom and dad made good money and went to church, but they were like most everyone else in their nice neighborhood—products of American culture, striving for the "American Dream." They believed in their faith and even sent money to missionaries and supported the programs at church. But week after week they sat in the pews singing about that day in the unclouded future when life would have some meaning.

No one seemed to recognize the message he was getting. It was the same at church, at home, at school: Life is meaningless. The only thing a Christian has to look forward to is getting out of this world...the sooner, the better.

The one-line note he left on his desk laid bare his confusion. It read: "If Heaven is my hope, I'm cashing in now."

The funeral had had the feel of hopelessness, and those left behind could not quite escape it. They felt the heaviness. All of them were dealing with the grief of losing a friend. Some of them were experiencing the questions of guilt: Had they been friendly, or had they been too self-absorbed to really reach out and know him? Had they ignored clues and pleas for help, or was it something no one could have foreseen or stopped? Guilt came with the former, but an even deeper fear came with the latter. Then again, what if he was right?

Unconsciously, but almost as one, they wandered to Uncle Herm's house.

Uncle Herm was their friend. Sort of a cross between a grandfather and a mentor, he was easy to know. He had an obvious love for young searching minds, and they trusted him because he was real. He encouraged their questions, but didn't mind saying, "I don't know." Herm was an elder in his local church where the other church leaders were fascinated by his affinity for "kids less than half his age" and encouraged his efforts to "father" these eager young seekers.

Don't get me wrong. Uncle Herm was no Mr. Rogers! There was a fierce determination in him. Although he had an easy sense of humor, he didn't suffer fools lightly. This was a man of firm conviction—a man with the wisdom of experience, the compassion of age, and the quiet confidence of a man who knows his God. He wasn't afraid to let them see his passion, and the kids liked that. He was anything but stodgy religious. Herm wasn't threatened by any question asked in sincerity, but would not mince words with anyone trying to pull religious shenanigans.

He was a veteran of war...a hero of sorts. He had served as a "radio man" during the Korean War, and had learned to speak the language in Vietnam, serving there also as an interpreter during the Vietnam War. After coming home, he had earned his theology degree from a respected seminary in the Midwest. Now he was content to focus on the few who could be difference-makers in the future.

The group had formed spontaneously. As a few friends would sit around and talk about things, a serious issue would emerge and someone would suggest, "Let's see what Uncle Herm thinks about that." Eventually they were meeting with him on a regular basis. It was informal and relaxed, and they talked about the things that mattered to them.

The group had no name until one day Chuck came rushing in with a frenzied look. He had been listening to some radio program, he told them. The host had proclaimed that events in the Middle East were ripe for the battle of Armageddon to begin right away. He was alarmed and couldn't believe everyone in the group wasn't ready to join him in running to the hills.

Chuck couldn't understand the others' lack of panic, and no matter where they tried to steer the discussion, he kept coming back to the battle of Armageddon. The next week, on her way to Uncle Herm's, Francis remarked that she was going to "The Armageddon Discussion." The name stuck. That had been several months ago and no battle had yet started in the valley of Jezreel. The discussion had moved on to many other subjects, but the group would always be "The Armageddon Discussion."

The Armageddon Discussion members each had different interests, but they were all bright, inquisitive seekers of truth. They had met through church and school and just running into each other as friends of friends. Despite their diversity, they recognized a commonality in each other. None of them was content with the passivity of a meaningless existence. They shared a sense of knowing there was something more and a hunger for finding true significance in life. So even when they got on each others' nerves—like Chuck hijacking the discussion for his moniker-giving Armageddon debates—they stuck with it.

Chuck was a conspiracy buff. No matter what was in the news, he was sure there was a sinister plot behind it. President Kennedy's assassination, Chuck insisted, was the result of an unlikely coalition of mafia bosses, Cuban communists, and international industrialists. Tall with dark hair and eyes, Chuck could go on for hours about the Illuminate, the Free Masons, the Trilateralists, and the Federal Reserve. He had read Nostradamus and the Bible Code. He loved prophecy prognosticators who used every newspaper headline to explain the fulfillment of Scripture. He was a good thinker, but truthfully, he would have preferred to debate the evil conspiracies at every discussion.

Francis was…well, glad to be saved. And that was it. She just didn't understand why all that other stuff was important.

Wasn't Jesus enough? It wasn't that she was afraid to think; she just preferred to avoid the divisions that emerged when the issues got deeper than the basics. "Who cares?" she would often say when the discussion got too technical— parsing Greek verbs or charting last-days timelines. "I just want to love Jesus and tell everyone about Him," she would say. She had a bit of the "let's just be nice and get along with everyone" mentality. She was certainly the most outgoing of the group, making friends with everyone she met. With her blonde hair and blue eyes, she sometimes had difficulty getting people to take her seriously. But she could be serious, and she was willing to tackle the tough questions when it was necessary. She just preferred that it not be necessary.

Kristy was a good church girl in the best sense of that phrase. Petite with a mop of bouncing brown curls, she was a joy to be around, always pleasant and willing to serve. She was the kind of girl everyone likes, but only those who take the time really get to know. Her dad had been a bit of a rebel back in his day, but had been converted in the 70's after reading Hal Lindsay's *Late Great Planet Earth*. As a result, Kristy grew up in the church and had a fairly good working knowledge of eschatology, though it, like most of her theology, was secondhand. She had heard it from Dad who heard it from Hal. Kristy knew the lingo and the Bible stories, but she was just beginning to think it all through and appropriate it as her own.

Paul, with his tousle of red hair, came to the group with a good understanding of theology and a distrust of radical new ideas. Paul didn't see any sense in rocking the theological boat. He was a true conservative—if the good men before us believed one way, then you better have a good reason to change it. Rarely the first to speak, Paul was a serious thinker whose comments carried the weight of careful analysis. He generally believed that differing positions on major issues were the result of bad communication. He just knew that if you got all the disagreeing parties together to talk it out, you could solve the problem. The Armageddon Discussion had just about destroyed that belief.

All in all they were an unlikely group just to hang out together, but they shared a hunger for truth and reality. These were kids who would make a difference. They were leaders—each in his or her own way. The differences of background and personality actually served to enrich the discussions.

Today, however, they all found themselves sitting on rocking chairs or the steps of Uncle Herm's porch contemplating and even sharing some of the despair Jason must have felt in the last few days before the crash. Uncle Herm had attended the funeral as well and was quite somber. As he pulled up a rocker and began to slowly move back and forth, he finally broke the silence. "It's important what you believe about the end. It's not just for discussion. It *does* affect the choices you make every day."

There was a long pause and then, "You know what really bothers me?" Everyone looked up now, expecting to receive another bit of Uncle Herm's heartfelt wisdom.

"I *expect* the world to preach a message of hopelessness. From the perspective of life without God, life is hopeless, meaningless, and confusing. But the Church should be the voice of ultimate hope, and not the kind that says you have to get out of here to get help. That message is no different than what the world says. Too much of the Church is promoting a message of fear and meaninglessness. That has gotta change! It's worth the pain of reformation to see that change."

Uncle Herm seemed to be talking to more than the few on the porch. Maybe he was talking to himself. Maybe he was making commitments inside as he spoke. One thing was for sure—he was serious. All the signs were there—furrowed brow, tight-pursed lips, and a faraway stare. He wasn't just discussing...he was making plans.

CHAPTER 2

In the End...We Fail?

"I just don't see how Jason could do it. How could it really have been *that* bad?" asked Francis. She paused, then asked quietly, "Do you think he's in Heaven?"

"How you die doesn't determine whether or not you go to Heaven," Uncle Herm answered thoughtfully. "Life can get real confusing—even for Christians —when truth is mingled with deception. But God is faithful to us even when we're weak...or perhaps I should say, *especially* when we're weak."

But Paul needed answers. "Is there something in our culture that's promoting the kind of hopelessness that gripped Jason? And what can we do to stop this kind of stuff?" Paul dropped his head. "Jason is the third person we know who has taken his own life. And we know dozens of others who have checked out but are still breathing. Some are on drugs, you know, but most are just hanging around wondering what they should do with their lives. A few hang around the church youth group wishing they were still young enough to be there. Maybe they're afraid of growing up and taking responsibility for their lives. I don't know...

"On the other hand, several of our friends are married and they seem kind of happy, I guess, but even they don't see much purpose other than making a living and raising their kids. I bet they even wonder what they're raising them for." Paul sighed. "Maybe I'm wrong. I hope so."

"I worry about my *parents*," Kristy chimed in. "They're wonderful people—don't get me wrong. But they seem to have lost the zest for living they used to have. They tell stories about the old days when they had to trust God for beans in the cupboard and when they both worked so they could buy gas to make a weekend visit to their parents. They laugh nostalgically about the adventurous struggles of their youth, but they don't seem to have heart for adventures in the future…except perhaps for their hopes of grandchildren, which puts a little pressure on unmarried me. I want to get married, I guess. But is life really all about bigger houses, IRA's, retirement, grandchildren, and Heaven? I wish they could enjoy the risks again."

"Well, all these are signs that the end is near," Chuck stated emphatically. "The Bible says that things will get worse and worse before the end comes. We should just 'lift up our heads for our redemption draws nigh.' Just the other day I heard a well-known prophet saying that the antichrist is alive and ready to make his move. All this terrorism and escalating wars just makes me want to get on the highest roof and wait for the air to split with the coming of Christ so He can judge this wicked old world and get us out of here."

"That might be part of the problem, Chuck," said Uncle Herm as he shifted in his chair. "Maybe too many of us have retreated to the housetops and left the managing of the cosmos to those who don't know its Creator."

"But isn't it true that the world is under the control of the devil and will only be destroyed by the burning wrath of God?" insisted Chuck. "That's what I've been told by several different Bible teachers."

"I think that premise could stand some reevaluation." Uncle Herm disagreed kindly. "The devil is in charge of the world of carnality, sure, but he doesn't have any right to claim ownership of the world. When Adam sinned, the world was cursed and

Adam lost the authority to subdue it; but the devil didn't become its creator or lord. He has his world—lust of flesh, lust of the eye, and pride of life. He's the father of lies and the original murderer, but he has no claim on God's world. And don't forget that the Last Adam regained the authority the first Adam lost. So we are not the inevitable victims of a devil-dominated world. We still have the assignment given to our first father to subdue the earth under God's guidance.

"By the way, do you know what the two mandates we live under are?"

"I'm not exactly sure what you mean," Paul said, "but I know we're to make disciples. And I guess from what you just said that the other is to subdue the earth? Whatever that means."

"Yes, those are the two mandates, and as far as I know, neither of them has been canceled. I think the Bible teaches that God made man to express the nature of God on earth by bringing 'cosmos' out of 'chaos.' He gave man the ability to manage the earth under His control and make it a shining expression of God's glory. That's what 'subdue the earth' means.

"When man fell to the temptation of the devil, he lost the fellowship with God needed to properly manage the earth, and began to use it for self-centered purposes. The curse of sin's destruction was spread to all of creation. But that's not the end of the story." Uncle Herm paused, his eyes shining.

"There is another Adam. He came to reclaim what the first Adam lost. After He had defeated the devil and paid the price of the broken commands, He gave authority to His disciples to get on with the project of managing the earth under the control of God's Kingdom. He spent 33 years showing what that would look like on earth. So when He said, 'Go make disciples!' what did He mean?"

"Well, He meant for us to go tell the gospel and get people to receive Christ as their Lord and Savior," Paul offered.

"And...?" Uncle Herm asked.

Paul continued quickly, "And get them in church and get them going about doing the same thing."

Uncle Herm kept pushing. "And what would be their job if all the people on earth received Christ and joined a church?"

Paul shrugged his shoulders. "Well, that's not going to happen, but I guess—theoretically—if it did, that would be the end."

"So what about the earth? Does God have any future for the created order?"

"It's going to burn up anyway, so why should we be concerned with it?" Chuck asked.

Uncle Herm was ready to fire. "Okay. Let's go over what you just told me. Basically, you're saying God has given us a job that we can't get done and we work on a planet that has no future? In other words, God has started a project that has been so marred by sin that the only thing left for it is total destruction. In the end, He's going to just burn it all up? Doesn't that sound to you like the devil wins? What did Jesus' death, resurrection, ascension, and sending the Holy Spirit mean in the big picture? Is our only victory in our ticket to Heaven? If our only hope is Heaven, then Jason wasn't all that confused."

Uncle Herm sat back in his rocker and looked around the group. The young people sat stunned, trying to evaluate what he had just said. Finally, Francis broke the silence.

"You know, a few nights ago I was watching a preacher on TV raising money for a school. He projected that it could be finished in two years. The kicker for me was he had just preached that the signs of the times indicated that Jesus would be back in the next few years. Now, why does he need a school if Jesus is coming back before he can educate the students or possibly before he can even get it built?"

"Sounds like maybe he doesn't totally believe what he's saying, huh?" said Uncle Herm. "You know, we tend to make fun of the 'fanatics' who sell their stuff and go to some mountain to wait for the end of the world. But at least they're consistent with what they say. I don't recommend that approach, however. Our mandate is to be occupying in the name of our conquering King until our time is up. I think we do a great disservice to people by leading them to believe that they can expect escape when things get rough. The life Jesus gave us can tackle the roughest challenges and still rejoice. We're not to be fearful of what the devil and the world can concoct. First John 5:4 says we are people of a faith who overcome the world."

Uncle Herm's Homework

1. What was the assignment for mankind originally? (See Genesis 1:26-28.) What would that look like today?

2. What authority does the devil have now in the universe?

3. What are the implications of our assignment in Matthew 28:18-20?

4. What gives you hope for a meaningful life?

CHAPTER 3

What Are We Thinking?

The Armageddon Discussion ended on a somber note since everyone was still reeling from the funeral. Uncle Herm suggested that everyone reflect on the blessing Jason had been and rejoice in his contribution to their lives. Everyone was assigned to make a "thanksgiving list" for grace they had seen in Jason's life.

"Hey, I don't want to stop here," said Kristy as everyone gathered their things to leave. "When we're feeling better I want to talk about this more. I've always thought the doctrines relating to the last days and the second coming of Christ were for preachers and theologians to discuss when they had nothing else to do."

"Well," Uncle Herm suggested, "why don't you all do a topic search through the New Testament on the Kingdom of God and the Kingdom of Heaven? Just find all the places those terms are used and try to get a definition of what it really is. We can talk about what you find next time."

Uncle Herm closed the door on the last of them and sank into his old recliner, his Bible close at hand. He couldn't help but think about Luke 24:13-49 describing the disciples on the Emmaus Road after the death of Jesus. He knew his kids were questioning what they believed, just like those men did of long ago. But when Jesus appeared on the road and explained the Old Testament and how it revealed Him, it brought a time of new understanding. Their hearts burned within them, according to their testimony. Maybe the death of Jason could be the springboard for a "heart burning" revelation for the Armageddon Discussion. It was certainly worth praying for.

More than a week went by before the Armageddon Discussion group could meet again. Francis was the last one to arrive at Uncle Herm's porch, but she was the first one to jump into the discussion.

"I thought it was really hard to get a definition of the Kingdom of God," she stated emphatically. "Even Jesus kept saying, 'The Kingdom of Heaven is like…' and then He'd tell a story. Maybe it's too big to put into words." She paused. "But I was surprised at how many times it's mentioned. I've been in church all my life and haven't heard much about the Kingdom except as a future kind of place."

Paul jumped in. "Yeah, but it actually seems to be the central theme of Jesus—like all He did was demonstrate the nature of the Kingdom of God. And Paul spent his last days talking about it too."

"Personally, I don't get it." Chuck interjected. "John the Baptist said it was near. Jesus said it was at hand and that seems to mean 'here,' yet things were not all that different—at least in the temporal world. Doesn't that just go to prove that God is not interested in the world? I think He is spiritual and only works in the spiritual realm."

Paul was uncomfortable with Chuck's analysis. "I think that gets too close to a dualism that could be dangerous. God has never been afraid of material. He made it, and in fact, God became a man who is material as well as spiritual."

"That's right," Uncle Herm agreed. "Dualistic thinking has led to many discouraging conclusions. The early Gnostics taught that material is evil and only the spiritual is good. Therefore, they denied that Jesus had really come in the flesh. They also concluded that since only the spiritual was valuable, it didn't matter what they did in the flesh. So, you can see how easy total irresponsibility is in that belief system. Today, this kind of thinking leads to the feeling among those who are not 'called' to church related ministries that they are second-class citizens. A Kingdom perspective would assure them that we are all called to do our part in subduing every sphere of the earth's domain and that all such work is holy. Look it up in Colossians 3:23-24. If only the 'spiritual' matters, then the earth is just a mud ball waiting to be burned up...and any work done here is valuable only if we learn spiritual lessons while doing it."

"But isn't it supposed to be in the millennium when the earth is restored?" Kristy asked. "I was taught that the kind of progress you're talking about could only happen during the millennium."

"That brings up an interesting topic," Uncle Herm mused. "Exactly what *does* the Bible say about the millennium?"

Chuck responded promptly. "It says that after the rapture of the believers and the time of tribulation Jesus will set up His throne in Jerusalem and rule the earth for one thousand years."

"Where does it say that, Chuck?" Kristy picked up her Bible, ready to read it for herself.

Chuck shrugged. "I don't know exactly, but I know it's in there."

"Actually, the thousand years, or millennium, is mentioned explicitly only once," Uncle Herm explained patiently. "In Revelation 20:6. We need to remember, though, that The Revelation is a book that fits the definition of apocalyptic literature. That means reality is depicted in symbols. To try to make it literal might possibly lead us to miss the point of the whole book. We should at least look for confirming texts in other parts of the New Testament. Instead, I think the Church may be suffering from a millennium virus."

"That's a term I've never heard," muttered Paul.

Uncle Herm smiled. "I went to our family doctor one time and he told me I had a virus. I reminded him that he had said that the last time I was sick, but my symptoms now were completely different. He confessed that when doctors don't know exactly what's wrong, they just throw it into the 'virus' bin, and try to eliminate the symptoms. That seems to be what the Church has done with many of the promises and provisions of the New Covenant. If we can't immediately see the manifestation of victory, we conclude that it's for the millennium. So we end up putting off to a tomorrow of speculation, the things we could enjoy today if we were to embrace them.

"But this isn't a new thing," Uncle Herm continued. "Remember how the people of Israel had looked forward to the 'promised land'? They had pictures in their mind of how it would look. They must have imagined that it would be something like Disney World. However, when they arrived at the edge of it and saw that it was occupied with giants, they were ready to put off the victory until it looked like what they had created in their own minds.

"It was the same when Jesus came. They had looked forward to the Messiah who would save them from their trouble, which they thought was political, economical, and geographical. When Jesus came riding on a donkey and associating with the poor, sick, and lonely they rejected Him. He did not fit their expectations and they put off the fulfillment of God's promises for them until a tomorrow filled with speculations.

"I think the entire focus of the New Testament is about the eternal life that Jesus made available now."

"But what about the second coming?" Chuck insisted. "Didn't Jesus talk a lot about that?"

"Did He, Chuck? As you read the New Testament, compare the clear, unmistakable references to the last coming of Christ with those explaining the purpose and benefits of the cross-event. I think you'll find that the climax of history is not in the end of existence, but in the revelation of God's Son as the center of all reality."

Uncle Herm paused to let his words sink in. All eyes were on him as he continued, his voice building with excitement as he spoke. "The first coming of Christ—including His unique birth, His life, death, resurrection, ascension, and coming in the person of the Holy Spirit—explains the meta-narrative, the story that explains the purpose of history. This is the climax of the story. Jesus doesn't have to wait until the end of time to be the Hope of Israel, the King sitting on David's throne, the Messiah, the ultimate Priest, the final Prophet, the fulfillment of Old Testament promises, and the Life. He is that now! We're not waiting for Jesus to be crowned as King. That's already done. We're not waiting for the defeat of the devil; according to John 12:31, Jesus has done that. Judgment came when the Judge set the bar. Anyone who does not receive Jesus as God's only Son and the fulfillment of His plan has judged himself."

Uncle Herm sat back to catch his breath. After a moment he added thoughtfully, "Another good study would be to read John chapters 13 through 17 and see how much Jesus talked about the coming of the Holy Spirit as the big event the disciples should anticipate. Jesus was very excited about what would happen in that 'coming.' "

"Are you saying that Jesus *isn't* coming again?" Chuck asked incredulously.

"No! That's not what I'm saying at all," Uncle Herm stated emphatically. "But I *am* saying that we have tended to overlook the impact of the first coming while we specu-late on the last coming. There are some 'comings' in between that are pretty significant, too. For instance, what coming do you think Jesus was referring to when He said, 'Some standing here will see the king coming in His glory' in Matthew 16:28?"

"This is getting too confusing," Francis wailed. "And I don't even *like* this topic. My aunt has been trying to get me to read some books that talk about the danger of being left behind when the rapture occurs. I've managed to put her off but I'm amazed at how popular these books are. They've sold millions of copies. Why is this subject so popular?"

Chuck answered with authority. "It's probably because it's so close to the end, and this hunger is a sign of the times. You know, with all the terrorist fears and economic instability around. And there are wars breaking out all over. I think it could be just another sign we should look up."

"Maybe Chuck, but there might be some less speculative answers, too," Uncle Herm said kindly. "First, people are natu-rally curious. Since the Garden of Eden, man has wanted to know as God knows, even when that knowledge is forbidden. We love to solve mysteries. And when we don't know, we're good at speculative theories. There are some things we can learn from observation, some that we can only learn by revela-tion, and some that God has hidden from us.

"Secondly, and more importantly, we all want meaning and somehow believe that if we could know the end of the story, we could find the meaning of it. It seems, though, that in our effort to find the end, we've missed the climax. Like I said earlier, the Bible is not focused on the end of existence, but the purposes of God. If we can't find meaning in the first coming of Christ, we won't find it in the end-time theories, no matter how firmly we defend them."

Francis was still confused. "But what about people being left behind when the rapture occurs? Do we still believe that?"

"I don't know what you believe now, Francis, but I think it's important that you find a worldview that releases you to become what you were designed to be. What we believe determines how we behave." Uncle Herm smiled at her gently. "It's not enough to leave the thinking to those who have nothing better to do than speculate. You have the Holy Spirit in you and the Bible in your hand. If your heart is open and you are willing to seek—which is spelled 'w-o-r-k'—for the truth, God will explain all you need to know in order for you to get done all you have been assigned. First Corinthians 2:9-16 is an excellent passage where you will find that His revelation is not just for the purpose of discussion, but He will open your eyes to see enough to joyfully fulfill your destiny."

"But at least tell us your opinion," Paul insisted. "Do you believe the thesis on being left behind?"

"It's not my opinion that matters," Uncle Herm said firmly. "So let's look in Luke 17:20-37. Here's a discourse by Jesus on the nature and presence of the Kingdom of God. In this discussion, Jesus is describing what is happening to Him and to those who follow Him. After His rejection by the religious establishment of the day, a judgment on that unbelieving generation will take place. God, using the instrument of a pagan army, will carry it out. By the way, He has done this several times in Israel's history. The exact time of the destruction is not revealed, but the certainty of it is emphasized. Those who have failed to recognize Him will carry on their normal lives without regard to the looming wrath that is shortly coming. The same blindness that kept them from seeing the Messiah in Jesus will keep them from seeing the alarming signs of their own destruction. Read Luke 19:42 also.

"Back to Luke 17, it seems clear to me that Jesus is describing the monumental and pivotal event of the destruction of Jerusalem in 70 AD. He refers to the times of Noah. I would like to mention that in the Flood, Noah was left behind—and glad. Jesus also spoke of Lot in the days of Sodom and Gomorrah. Lot was not destroyed. He was left behind—and glad. Not only were they glad, but they were left behind with the purpose of starting over with the mandate to subdue. I think the emphasis we should look for is purpose. We need to know the reason we're here and what we should be doing while we're here.

"It's true that in the destruction of Jerusalem the believers were saved by leaving the city just as Lot did in his day. In that sense they were rescued while the wicked were left to be destroyed. But they were left to continue to fulfill the mandate and finish the job they were given.

"The emphasis on being rescued and leaving the world to be destroyed is an irresponsible emphasis. It doesn't do justice to the redeeming work of Jesus who has given us all the necessary equipment to be victorious in the world. It shortchanges the power of the cross and the resurrection. We are not victims of a world gone bad. Instead, we are ambassadors of a Kingdom that is so powerful it can change even the vilest man or nation. We have a message so full of hope it can create faith that not only moves mountains, but also transforms cultures.

"So, you can see where I stand. I'm not looking for the rescue that pulls us out just before we cave in. I'm looking for the power of the life that has already been given to us by the grace of God in Christ Jesus."

"Wow! This is pretty radical!" Kristy exclaimed. "I've never heard any of this. Are you the only one who believes this way?"

"I can assure you that there are many who believe the same way I do," Uncle Herm smiled. "Not everyone buys into the pre-millennial dispensational views of eschatology."

"Maybe you'd better explain dispensational eschatology," Paul added, "for those in the group who don't know what it means."

"Good idea, Paul," said Uncle Herm. "Eschatology is the term we use to describe the study of the end, or the last days. Dispensational pre-millennialism is the term commonly used to refer to a branch of eschatology that was popularized by John Nelson Darby who lived from 1800-1882, and C.I. Scofield, 1843-1921. It embraces several key points.

"First, time is divided into seven different periods of time, or dispensations.

"Second, when the Jews rejected the Kingdom presented by Jesus, a new dispensation, which was hidden in the Old Testament, began. It was the parenthesis of the church age.

"Third, the prophecy clock stopped then and will be restarted only when the church age is concluded by its rapture.

"Fourth, God will then work through Israel again, and Jerusalem will be the center of political and religious activity on the earth.

"Fifth, the temple will be rebuilt and sacrifices restored. And of course, Israel will be fully restored.

"Some people make a major point of seeing Israel as the key to God's purposes and believe that all nations will be judged by how they respond to national Israel. Therefore political influence is garnered to insure that our nation is in line with Israel. Those who believe this theology see the next big event on God's calendar as the rapture of the Church. This will allow the clock to start again moving toward the final days of history, which include a millennial reign, a literal battle of Armageddon, and final judgment.

"There is actually a modified version of original pre-millennialism that sees the modern birth of Israel as a nation in 1948, as the starting of the prophecy clock. That was part of the argument of Hal Lindsay's *Late Great Planet Earth*. He speculated that the budding of the fig tree mentioned by Jesus in Matthew 24:32-35 was the establishment of Israel as a nation. He predicted that within a generation of that event the last of the last days would arrive and the end would come. But 1988 came and went and reinterpretations have been spawning new books. New dates are suggested that keep the reader expecting the end to come with each day's newspaper headline."

"This is not getting any clearer," Francis fretted. "Is there something I can read that will help?"

"Francis, I'm glad you asked!" smiled Uncle Herm.

Uncle Herm's Homework

1. Read from at least one of the following:

   The New Millennium Manual by Clouse, Hosack, and Pierard (Baker Book House).

   The Last Days Are Here Again by Kyle (Baker Book House).

   Last Days Madness by Gary DeMar (American Vision).

   Last Days According to Jesus by R.C. Sproul (Baker Book House).

2. Using your concordance, read each Scripture that includes "Kingdom of God" or "Kingdom of Heaven."

3. Study the parables of the Kingdom in Matthew chapter 13.

4. If you had been among the original disciples listening to Jesus teach, what would you have concluded?

CHAPTER 4

Call No Man Teacher

"Maybe the most important thing we could discuss is the need for each believer to hear the word of God," Uncle Herm said as he started out the next meeting of the Armageddon Discussion. Rain poured down outside as the group gathered around Uncle Herm's fireplace.

"Why is that the most important thing?" Francis asked as she hung her dripping raincoat by the door and joined the group by the fire.

"The reason wrong emphases and even wrong doctrine can get strongholds in the Church is that we neglect our privilege to hear God's word to us," Uncle Herm explained. "I know I'm guilty. For most of my life I avoided the study of eschatology. It all seemed too complicated and I was more interested in practical studies. I spent most of my time studying the 'red letters' in the Gospels and the 'therefores' in the Epistles. I had simply decided to leave eschatology to the prophecy experts and concentrate on more 'important issues.' So, I essentially gave up my right to find truth and simply bought whatever was being sold.

"I read Hal Lindsay's *Late Great Planet Earth* when it first came out. His system of interpretation was different from mine, but I really tried to buy into his prophetic scheme. In the end I couldn't. The point is: I didn't have an eschatology and was vulnerable to someone who did. I think that's why so many people bought into the pre-millenial dispensational view. C.I. Scofield put his views in the notes of a King James Version of the Bible. As people read the Scriptures, they only had to look at the bottom of the page to get his biased view. To those who had no view, his was a welcome one.

"Jesus told His disciples that they were to call no man 'teacher.' Have you ever thought about what that means?"

"I've thought about it," Paul volunteered. "I just never reached an explanation that was totally comfortable."

"It all comes down to this," Uncle Herm said earnestly. "He is the only one who can fully explain truth." He paused to let it sink in. "Now certainly, God has given teachers to the Church in order to help them hear the word of the Teacher. These are individual members with the gift of teaching, and this gift *is* from God. But when other humans become the final explanation, they have usurped a place Jesus reserves for Himself. That's why I don't want to become another teacher who replaces the voice of your real Teacher. I'll try to stimulate your hunger and facilitate your search, but I can't give you revelation."

Uncle Herm stretched out his toes toward the fire. "Now I'm as lazy as you, and I'd be happy for someone to just tell me what to believe. But that would invite false doctrine and insult my Teacher. He longs to develop the relationship that comes with my learning from Him.

"You should be aware that most people have simply adopted a view by default. It was the view of someone they admired or it was the one they were taught before they were consciously seeking the truth. They shouldn't be blamed. It's a good trait to trust those who lead us. Don't fret or condemn people for what they were taught. Those committed to truth will hear the truth and recognize it because they have the Holy Spirit and He witnesses to truth. It's the teachers who will be held more accountable for lack of diligence in high-lighting the truth.

"Let's seek to find the heart of our Teacher and become lovers of Truth. We don't need to find a theological position out of reaction. We believe real freedom comes from knowing the truth."

"But, that makes it seem too hard." Francis was fretting again. "How can we ever know the right things to believe? How do we have an objective view of Scripture?"

"That's our goal!" Uncle Herm smiled. "Actually, an objective view is sort of a misnomer. All of us come to the Scriptures with presuppositions. That is, we all have some kind of 'glasses' through which we view everything. That's why there are so many views defended with different interpretations of Scripture. Our goal is to submit to the view of reality as defined by Jesus. If His lordship means anything, it means He has a right to define our perspective.

"Those whose hearts are more bent to expecting the worst to happen, find it easy to explain life and Scripture in terms of looming judgment. There are lots of angry prophets out there. Maybe they're angry at what has been dealt to them in life and are hoping God will destroy the whole scene. Maybe they're like Jonah and don't want God to be gracious to their enemies. You remember him, don't you?"

"Oh, sure, it was a whale of a tale," Chuck punned. "But seriously," he added, as the others rolled their eyes and groaned, "is that why Jonah disobeyed God? He didn't want the people of Nineveh to be forgiven?"

"That's right," said Uncle Herm. "Jonah knew God was full of mercy, and if the Ninevites gave Him a chance, He would suspend judgment and forgive them. I think there are lots of Jonah-types still around.

45

"Remember that Jesus said something very important about 'seeing' in the famous passage in John chapter 3. 'Unless one is born again he cannot *see* the Kingdom of God' (Jn. 3:3b, emphasis added). Seeing is so important! The apostle Paul prayed in Ephesians 1:17-18 that the eyes of our heart would be opened and that we would have the Spirit of wisdom and revelation in the knowledge of Him. It's difficult to change the pictures in our mind, but that is the essence of repentance. Until we change what we see, we won't permanently change our behavior.

"You know how you feel when you've looked long and hard at some hologram and finally see the real picture. I think that's what happened to Paul (or Saul) on the road to Damascus. When he finally saw that Jesus was the fulfillment of Old Testament prophecies, promises, and types, he was changed. It all made sense in a whole new way. He died for the truth he saw in the new picture. None of us wants to die defending the wrong picture. Our sincere prayer is that we can see through the eyes of truth.

"Don't be fooled by the demand for objectivity. None of us has it. A relatively recent theologian, Cornelius Van Til, made a great contribution to modern thought by emphasizing the power of presuppositions. You may have heard it said like this: 'The mind justifies what the heart embraces.' Bad philosophy comes from a bad heart. We want something badly enough to justify the thoughts needed to make it acceptable. Atheists don't believe in hell, not because they have good empirical evidence against it, but because they don't want to change their beliefs to avoid it. Once we accept a system of assumptions, we bend everything in observation, history, and even Scripture to fit the system. So you see, there's no room for arrogance in the search for truth. Only the contrite in heart will receive the true pictures of reality, as it says in Psalm 51:17.

"That doesn't mean we shouldn't *try* to be objective. We can all ask for the spirit of revelation and wisdom as we approach the Scriptures. By the way, do you know the vital key in interpreting the Scriptures?"

"No, what?" asked Paul.

"We'll talk about that next time, after you've had the chance to do a little reading. But I promise you one thing," Uncle Herm's eyes twinkled. "It's more important than you think."

Uncle Herm's Homework

1. Read Luke 24:13-49.

2. Why did Jesus give such priority after His resurrection to explaining Old Testament Scriptures?

3. What were the keys to their finally "seeing" the
   truth?

4. If you had been there, what would you have
   learned that day?

5. Compare Luke 24:13-49 with Matthew 23:8-12
   and First John 2:20-21,26-27.

CHAPTER 5

The Greatest Bible Class

Uncle Herm put his car in park and smiled at the group already gathered on his front porch. He was running a bit late, but couldn't resist the urge to pause and reflect on his little flock. They really were growing up, spiritually speaking. He could tell that they were getting more interested in finding answers for themselves. And they were finally beginning to recognize that thoughts about the future do affect daily choices. He couldn't be more proud of them. He was also aware that they thought they knew how to interpret Scripture, but they had just enough doubt to make them want to listen to what he had to say.

He joined the group amid a flurry of greetings and good-natured teasing. It was a glorious fall day, brisk but sunny, and much too beautiful to be indoors. Uncle Herm settled into his favorite rocker on the porch and asked them what their home-work had revealed.

"I read the passage in Luke 24," Francis began. "I wish I had been in *that* Bible study. I mean—it was like the 'Word' teaching the Word."

"When it says that He showed them all things written about Him in the Law of Moses, the Prophets, and the Psalms, does that mean He just took every verse that referred to Him and explained it in light of Himself?" Chuck asked.

"I think it was even more than that." Uncle Herm settled further into his chair and into his subject. "He was saying that the whole Old Testament was about Him. It wasn't just the scattered verses that might refer to Him amidst all other Scripture. He was the theme and subject of all of history. He is not only the author; He is the main character in the story that gives meaning to history."

Kristy was amazed. "Does every verse of the Old Testament refer to Jesus?"

"I don't think that's what Uncle Herm is saying," Paul explained patiently. "There are obviously verses that speak about other subjects, but the theme of it all is to point to Jesus."

"Have any of you ever been bothered by the moralistic approach to Scripture?" asked Uncle Herm.

"A moralistic approach?" Kristy raised her eyebrows.

"A moralistic approach is where we reduce every story down to some principle or lesson," Uncle Herm explained.

"Sounds like when we were kids in Sunday school," Francis laughed.

"Yeah, I remember going to church and hearing Bible stories with the bottom line of being a good little boy," said Paul. "Like one time, my teacher taught about Abraham lying about Sarah being his wife. He said she was his sister because he didn't want to be killed. But I noticed that God blessed Abraham a lot and made him a very rich and influential man. That didn't seem to be a good lesson on lying."

Everyone laughed.

"Well, you may have a point," smiled Uncle Herm. "But let's look at it another way. What is the message in the biblical story of David?"

Kristy wrinkled up her nose. "Well, you've got me a little skeptical now, but I've always been taught that it was about courage and faith. We can stand against the enemies of God today if we have the faith and courage of David."

"Where is Jesus in the story?" Uncle Herm asked.

"He's pictured in David, I guess," Francis answered.

"Right." Uncle Herm nodded. "Certainly there's value in the faith and courage of David as it relates to us, but the story is about a deliverer. Unimpressive to the natural eye, disqualified by his own brothers, the unexpected deliverer comes to fight the enemy of God and save the destiny of God's people. Sound like anyone we know?"

Everyone nodded.

"Don't get me wrong. This is not just a selected event out of history that contains a reflection of Jesus. It is a real story about God preserving a people through whom He would redeem the world. The Old Testament is vital to the full revelation of God's nature. Without David, no son of David; no son of David, no Messiah."

Uncle Herm continued. "If we go away from the story with just some principles and miss Jesus, we'll be doomed to the futility of trying to improve ourselves by our own efforts. If we can see Jesus, then we find grace to express faith and courage since He now lives in us to work through us."

"So our task is to find Jesus in the Scriptures?" Francis wanted to know.

"Let's just say that until we see Him, we haven't seen the fullness of the revelation intended for that passage," Uncle Herm clarified. "From Genesis to Revelation, Jesus is the feature. When the Bible is reduced to lessons about life, or answers to man's questions, or predictions about future events, we miss the point."

Kristy was still confused. "I always thought the Old Testament was about Israel and the New Testament was about Jesus."

"Well, that's true to a certain extent," Chuck said confidently. "God gave Israel a chance to be His people, but they failed, so He started over with Jesus and the disciples. At least that's what I've always thought."

"That's a common understanding, Chuck," Uncle Herm said gently. "But I believe it's a great deal more majestic than that."

Chuck threw up his hands in mock surrender. "Okay. I'm all ears. What's the story?"

"God has no alternative plans." Uncle Herm paused to let that thought sink in. Then he jumped in with both feet. "God has always designed that Jesus be glorified in the earth. God the Father has such delight in Jesus the Son that He created mankind to delight in Him too. Man's fall was an opportunity for the eternal mercy of God to be expressed through the Son."

He leaned forward in his chair. "When God clothed Adam and Eve with skins from slain animals, He was pointing toward Jesus. When He gave Israel the covenant at Sinai, He was preparing a people for a Deliverer. The whole sacrificial system of the Old Testament was pointing to Jesus. The prophecies of redemption spoke of Jesus the Redeemer. David the king pointed to Jesus who would one day fulfill the covenant God had made with David. Jesus is the 'Son' who sits today on the throne of David governing the Kingdom of God. The restoration promised by the prophets of the Exile was a prediction of Jesus' resurrection. Every deliverance story in the Old Testament speaks of Jesus. Every true prophecy speaks of Him. Every good king foretells His Kingdom. Every poem of the psalmist and proverb of the wise men speak of Him. Every song expresses His glory and every prayer is an expressed hope in His mercy."

"Wow!" Kristy's eyes were wide.

"That is cool," Paul agreed. "I like looking at it from that perspective. But what does that mean to us when we are trying to interpret the Scriptures?"

"It means that Jesus is the final arbiter of any interpretation," Uncle Herm said. "His life and words are truth. All theories are to be measured by Him. The story begins with Him and ends with Him. All Scripture must be interpreted in light of where it fits into His story."

Kristy was thoughtful. "Well, if the New Testament is the fulfillment of the Old Testament, shouldn't we just study the New Testament and leave the Old alone?"

"No! Not at all." Uncle Herm was adamant. "But it *does* mean that we should let substance interpret shadows rather than the reverse. Many people read the Bible like an Old Testament person, and they interpret the New Testament in light of the Old. That will produce all kinds of confusion. For instance, look at the issue of Israel's land promise. If we ignore the New Testament—which does not mention the restoration of any land to Israel—and read the Old Testament as Israel being the center of attention, we will at best share the glory of Jesus with a speculated restoration of natural Israel.

"Or another popular example is viewing the grace revealed in the New Testament as a way to enable us to obey the Torah—the Old Testament Law. The focus is still on the Law, with Jesus coming to help us keep it. The New Testament reveals that the Law exposes our need of a Deliverer and is fulfilled in the shared life of Jesus. When we operate focused on the love He shares with us, the Law is fulfilled without our even being aware of it."

"Then what value is the Old Testament?" Paul asked. "Couldn't we get by with just the New?"

"No, there's great value in the Old Testament. It shows that all of history is about God's consistent plan to glorify Himself. There is great continuity in the Bible. To see the hand of God moving throughout history gives us more reason to worship. For us to read only the New Testament would be like reading just the last paragraph of a children's story. 'The frog became a prince and they lived happily ever after.' Okay. I want to know the rest of the story. Who lived happily? How did he become a prince? What's the point? Of course, I can know Jesus as Savior without the Old Testament, but there wouldn't be a Savior if not for what happened in the Old Testament. And why wouldn't I want to know the whole story?"

"I know we've talked before about the phenomena of the various interpretations of Scripture," began Francis. "I think that's led to people concluding that since there are so many different opinions, there's no final one. Their response is just 'whatever it means to me is the issue.' This does eliminate arguments: However you decide to read the Bible is fine because no one really knows what it means."

"Well, if it doesn't get personal, it will be dry Bible study," Chuck interjected. "I've sat in on some pretty dull Bible classes when they were discussing the technical aspects of interpretation. When I read the Bible, I want to know what God is saying to *me*."

"I agree, Chuck," Uncle Herm nodded. "There's a wide difference in academic Bible study and getting life from God's Word. But sometimes we try to bypass a vital step in interpretation."

"What's that?" Chuck asked.

"The Bible is not a magic book. It was written by the inspiration of the Holy Spirit through men who lived at specific periods of history with real-life circumstances prompting a revelation from God. Though God is transcendent and His word is transcendent, He spoke to real people in real life. If we are to get the best revelation from Scripture, we'll find it to be consistent with what was said in those situations. To take words God used to speak to the people of Moses' day and make them mean something different today for us is, at best, revisionism.

"Though the Holy Spirit can speak to us through any Scripture, He will not violate the integrity of the medium He chose to reveal Himself. God can reveal Himself any way He chooses. He has chosen to use people, history, language, and cultures to express Himself. If we really want to understand His revelation to us through Scripture, we'll get acquainted with the means He uses.

"It is important to realize that the Bible is not written 'to us' but 'for us.' However, God's word comes to us through the Scriptures. There's a dynamic in Scripture interpretation that goes beyond the natural mind interpreting a book. Notice how this works in First Corinthians 2:10-16:

> *These things God has revealed to us through the Spirit. For the Spirit searches everything, even the depths of God. For who knows a person's thoughts except the spirit of that person, which is in him? So also no one comprehends the thoughts of God except the Spirit of God. Now we have received not the spirit of the world, but the Spirit who is from God, that we might understand the things freely given us by God. And we impart this in words not taught by human wisdom but taught by the Spirit, interpreting spiritual truths to those who are spiritual. The natural person*

does not accept the things of the Spirit of God, for they are folly to him, and he is not able to understand them because they are spiritually discerned. The spiritual person judges all things, but is himself to be judged by no one. For who has understood the mind of the Lord so as to instruct Him? But we have the mind of Christ.

"I don't think this passage justifies anyone placing a subjective revelation over an obvious revelation in Scripture. But it does show us the difference in interpretation by the natural mind and the interpretation of the natural mind aided by the illumination of the Spirit. Some scholars would contend that interpretation is solely a matter of applying principles of interpretation common to all writing. They would argue that only in application does the Spirit give aid. I disagree. I believe there is good reason to expect the Spirit to be involved in the interpretation as well as the application, but that He honors the historical context in which the Word was given."

"So basically you're saying that we need to interpret all Scripture in light of its historical setting first," Kristy paraphrased. "I'm beginning to see why that would be important. But does that take the devotional dynamic out of the experience? Like...can I still read the Psalms and use them as my own prayers?"

"Of course," nodded Uncle Herm. "Actually, being familiar with the historical setting will *add* to your devotional use of Scripture. You'll also remove the nagging doubt about your tendency to read into Scripture what you want instead of what God actually says. Remember, the whole Book is one story, and each part fits into that story. It's not a collection of laws, ideas, tidbits of wisdom, parables, poems, and proverbs."

"I've tried to be a good student of Scripture by being faithful to look up words and make sure I'm getting the right translations," Paul added modestly. "I use lots of Greek and Hebrew word-study helps. What else do I need to do?"

"Word studies are very helpful...but only *after* some historical study," said Uncle Herm. "The first question we should ask is: In which covenant is the passage—old or new? We should know the purposes and distinctives of that covenant.

"Second question: What kind of literature is the passage? Each genre of literature has its own special personality. Is the passage historical, poetic, prophetic, apocalyptic, wisdom literature, etc.?

"Many people give more dignity to their reading of the daily newspaper than to Scripture. Someone reads the front page and learns that lions attacked some ranchers in Montana. The ranchers are badly injured and end up in the hospital. The reader has some feeling of compassion. He then turns to the sports page and reads that the Tigers killed the Cowboys. The reader either rejoices, mourns, or yawns. It was a football game. Then he turns to the editorial section and argues with the opinions of the writer. He might later read the comics and laugh. All of these are interpreted in light of the kind of literature. But that same reader might pick up the Bible and read from all kinds of literature and treat it the same. He will be focused on beasts coming out of the sea and signs in the heavens with as much fervor as he looks for the mandate for new covenant living in the Sermon on the Mount."

Now Paul was nodding. "I know what you mean. I heard a preacher on TV quoting from all over the Bible and putting the verses together to back up his point. He made no difference between the symbols and literal events. It was like 'Hamburger Bible.' You could actually make the Bible say anything with that approach."

"And unfortunately, many people do just that," said Uncle Herm sadly. "But the next question you need to ask is this:

What is the purpose of the Book that contains the passage? There is a reason for which each Book in the Bible was written. It's important to understand that purpose in order to get the context for the passage.

"Next, we want to know where in the flow of thought is the focal passage. *Now* we're ready to study the words. Once we know the setting, we're prepared to examine the words used by this author in line with his/her thoughts.

"I've seen word studies get people in trouble when they don't do their prior work. They find that in a concordance a word can be used several different ways. They choose one, disregarding the context, and end up making the passage say something totally different than the author intended."

"Can you give an example?" Chuck asked.

"Since we've been talking about issues of eschatology, I'll use one in Matthew 24," Uncle Herm replied. "In this passage Jesus is answering the question put to Him by the disciples regarding the destruction of the temple. He had told them that it would be totally destroyed and they were astounded. They wanted to know when. He gives several things they are to look for and some warnings about the coming events. He then says in Matthew 24:34 that these things will happen in 'this generation.' Some have noted that 'generation' could be translated 'race.' That would mean that the things Jesus warned about could happen before the race disappeared. That would allow for them to be projected into a speculated future. Actually, Matthew uses 'generation' several times, and each time, it is used to denote the people living at that time. Compare Matthew 23:36 to 11:16. It would be very strange for Jesus to use the same word and mean two different things when answering a time related question. This means that the events Jesus warned about were to happen in the next few years. They did. Jerusalem was attacked and the temple was destroyed in 70 A.D."

"I can see how we could use word studies to better fit our predetermined beliefs if we aren't careful," Paul said thoughtfully.

"It would be great if we all could believe that the truth is best for us. Then we could let the Bible say what it says and we would agree. But we all have pet beliefs that are difficult to subordinate to truth," said Uncle Herm. "Humility is a great aid to interpretation."

"It seems to me that prophecy is the most controversial kind of Scripture," Chuck stated. "How should we approach it?"

"The New Testament gives us the key," Uncle Herm explained. "On the day of Pentecost, Peter says that what is happening there is a fulfillment of what Joel prophesied. Read Acts 2:14-21:

> *But Peter, standing with the eleven, lifted up his voice and addressed them, "Men of Judea and all who dwell in Jerusalem, let this be known to you, and give ear to my words. For these men are not drunk, as you suppose, since it is only the third hour of the day. But this is what was uttered through the prophet Joel: 'And in the last days it shall be, God declares, that I will pour out My Spirit on all flesh, and your sons and your daughters shall prophesy, and your young men shall see visions, and your old men shall dream dreams; even on My male servants and female servants in those days I will pour out My Spirit, and they shall prophesy. And I will show wonders in the heavens above and signs on the earth below, blood, and fire, and vapor of smoke; the sun shall be turned to darkness and the moon to blood, before the day of the Lord comes, the great and magnificent day. And it shall come to pass that everyone who calls upon the name of the Lord shall be saved.' "*

"This was a shock to the people. What they had interpreted in the natural was fulfilled literally in the spiritual. These were the last days prophesied by Joel. Look at another insightful passage, Acts 3:24-26:

> *And all the prophets who have spoken, from Samuel and those who came after him, also proclaimed these days. You are the sons of the prophets and of the covenant that God made with your fathers, saying to Abraham, "And in your offspring shall all the families of the earth be blessed." God, having raised up His servant, sent Him to you first, to bless you by turning every one of you from your wickedness.*

"The apostle Peter concurs with this conclusion in First Peter 1:10-12:

> *Concerning this salvation, the prophets who prophesied about the grace that was to be yours searched and inquired carefully, inquiring what person or time the Spirit of Christ in them was indicating when he predicted the sufferings of Christ and the subsequent glories. It was revealed to them that they were serving not themselves but you, in the things that have now been announced to you through those who preached the good news to you by the Holy Spirit sent from heaven, things into which angels long to look.*

"The Old Testament prophets spoke of a coming day when God's promises to His people would be fulfilled. The New Testament says that day came with Jesus. Any prophecy that is not fulfilled in Jesus is alien to the New Testament writers. If a New Testament author doesn't comment on Old Testament prophecy, we are speculating to conclude it speaks of something other than that which relates to Jesus' coming as Incarnate God."

"What about the phenomena of dual or double fulfillment?" asked Paul, the budding theologian.

"I'm getting confused again," Kristy fretted. "What on earth is double fulfillment?"

Uncle Herm smiled sympathetically. "In the Old Testament, there were prophesies that had a fulfillment in that historical setting and yet were further fulfilled in Jesus. An example would be Isaiah's prophecy in Isaiah 7:10-17 about a young maiden (virgin) conceiving and bringing forth a son. It was a sign for that day, but was finally fulfilled in Jesus being born of a virgin. Again, let me remind you that Jesus is the final fulfillment of all prophecy. For us to interpret future fulfillments of prophecies that are not explained by inspired authors is to speculate. Many of the wild explanations of world events at any given time are said to be fulfilling prophecies.

"After an event fulfilled an Old Testament prophecy, New Testament authors recognized and explained it. If we follow that pattern, we'll have to wait until any unfulfilled prophecy is fulfilled and then the explanation would need to come from someone with the same kind of inspirational authority as a New Testament author."

"Wow!" Kristy was intrigued. "So that could be the answer to why all throughout history people have interpreted some Scriptures as being fulfilled in their day."

"We all like to think that we are the generation of focus," Uncle Herm said slowly. "But it's a bit presumptuous for us to believe it's all about us and concludes with us, don't you think? We live in the greatest days of history, but not because we're the terminal generation. We are the beneficiaries of God's fulfilled promises to His people. We can live with confident hope in the victory won for us by the ultimate David who defeated the ultimate enemy of God's ultimate people."

"I've read some Bible commentators that use a metaphor of Old Testament prophets looking forward and seeing a large mountain," Paul noted. "As time passed, it was recognized as a mountain range with several peaks. These different peaks could represent separate events in history but still be consistent with the purpose of the prophecy. For instance, those events in Matthew 24 primarily refer to the destruction of Jerusalem, but they could also refer to future events at the end of the world. What do you think about that?"

"The final mountain in the range is Jesus," Uncle Herm stated firmly. "He is the highest peak giving the final and best perspective. This mountain is about His promised coming in humility, His unmatched life, His sacrificial death, His victorious resurrection, His majestic ascension to the right hand of the Father, His gracious sending of the Holy Spirit, His continual reign as David's Son in the Kingdom of God, His guarantee that all injustice will be swallowed up in either mercy or judgment, and His final consummation of all things in His glory. If His answer to the disciples' questions regarding the destruction of the temple includes a future destruction for the earth, we will have to wait for another explanation from Him to get it straight. In the Old Testament, fuller manifestations are so unexpected they must be explained after the fulfillment."

"That's it." Chuck threw up his hands comically. "I need to throw away some of my modern prophecy books."

Everyone laughed. Then Francis added, "But seriously, Uncle Herm, why do so many insist on the conspiracy aspects of future events?"

"That's a good question." Uncle Herm glanced at his watch, then added ruefully, "But that will have to wait for another day!"

Uncle Herm's Homework

See if you can find a common theme regarding the relationship of the old and new covenants.

1. Read Peter's sermon in Acts 2:14-41.

2. What is his point in quoting Joel's prophecy?

3. When did he say the last days would be?

4. What are the main elements of the gospel proclaimed here? (List at least five.)

5. Read Acts 3:11-26.

6. How does this passage help us understand the relationship of the Old to the New Testament?

7. Read and compare Paul's sermons in Acts 13:16-47; 17:22-31; 21:27-28; 24:10-21; 26:1-23; 28:17-28.

CHAPTER 6

Who Is Israel?

Each member of the group went home with some new thoughts and a new curiosity. For perhaps the first time, they realized that they needed to give attention to *how* they were thinking as well as *what* they were thinking. Maybe well-meaning leaders had transferred some ideas that were not altogether true to Scripture. Uncle Herm was helping them see that equipped Christians are not people who have been told what to believe, but people who have learned to fellowship with the One who is the Truth.

More than a week passed before the next gathering. During the break, they took Uncle Herm's advice to study some material they hadn't known existed before. They also began to look more closely at Scriptures that everyone had always assumed referred to the end of time. When the group finally got back together, discussion was lively.

Paul went first. "I got a letter this week suggesting that everyone write their congressman and insist that Israel be given special political status because as a nation we would be blessed if we bless Israel, but cursed if we didn't. You mentioned that earlier. Is that right?"

"I've heard that, too." Kristy chimed in. "We've got several books at our house that make a big issue out of Israel being the key to end-time prophecy. They say that we should keep a keen eye on the events now in Israel, because God is committed to them, and we don't want to go against God."

"I was talking to one of my friends about this and told him some of the stuff we had discussed here," Chuck added. "He said that we sounded anti-Semitic."

Uncle Herm nodded. "I got one of those letters too, Paul. And Chuck, I know how easy it is to dismiss honest discussion of Israel by labeling ideas as anti-Semitic. So let's talk about Zionism for a while. Sadly, many have made Zionist doctrine the standard by which both political and theological ideas are to be judged. Anyone not agreeing with this narrow view is too quickly called anti-Semitic. Of course, all the emotional baggage that comes from the memory of the atrocities of Hitler's Nazism clutters the landscape of honest discussion. No one can justify what was done to Jewish people by that demonized ideology, but we can't make up for it by improperly elevating national Israel above Jesus and His universal Kingdom.

"Zionism as it affects Christian thought is relatively young. One of the cornerstone personalities was William Blackstone (1870). He had accepted the beliefs of John Nelson Darby, who I mentioned before. Blackstone took the lead, seeking to speed up the end-time prophecy clock by getting Jews back into their own land so the end-time scenario could take place. He believed that the Bible taught that Palestine belonged to the Jews. He produced a document known as the Blackstone Petition of 1891 and got some of the most important people of that day to sign it.

"In 1917, another document was produced that probably did more to determine the current situation. The Balfour Declaration from Britain ultimately led to the establishment of the State of Israel in 1948. Land that was occupied by Palestinians was declared Israel's. It can be argued that the guilt of the atrocities of World War II was a big factor in this move.

Also, there was still enough real anti-Semitism in Europe to want the Jews out of their land and into one of their own. Regardless of the different political motives involved in this action, I think the pre-millennial dispensational views of prophecy played a large role. Those who believed that a literal fulfillment of Israel's political restoration was necessary before there could be the final battle of Armageddon, wanted to get things in place quickly. They saw the establishment of Israel as a nation as a giant step in fulfilling biblical prophecy. They were glad to be used to get that done. Now, for them, the time clock was ticking again. Soon events would escalate and the time would quickly come for the big event—the rapture.

"It's regrettable that we tend to dismiss those we disagree with by lumping them into an emotionally charged and condemned category like anti-Semitic. The word actually means 'hatred or prejudice against Jews.' To believe that Israel is a recognized nation and has rights that all nations have is correct and good. But to say that Israel does not have to play by the same rules of justice and respect as other nations and that it can expect God to protect it regardless of any faith in Him is not. There is no evidence in Scripture that God promises to bless unbelieving Israel—ever.

"If Paul says to us, 'I am God!' and we all say, 'No, we don't believe you are God, Paul'; and Paul replies by saying, 'Then you are all atheists'; is that correct? No. Just because we don't believe Paul is God, doesn't make us atheists. And just because we don't believe that ethnic Jews have superior standing with God, doesn't make us anti-Semitic."

Chuck wasn't convinced. "What about that verse that says God will bless those who bless Israel and curse those who curse it?"

"I think you'll find those words are spoken to Abram by God in Genesis 12:3: 'I will bless those who bless you, and him who dishonors you I will curse, and in you all the families of the earth shall be blessed.'

"The question then becomes: Who are the people of Abraham? Throughout the Old Testament they were known as the Jews. Even then, however, God always blessed and identified with the believing Jews. Not all of Abraham's natural descendants were a part of the people of God. Remember 'Jacob I loved; Esau I hated.' The New Testament makes it clear that God has always defined His people by faith, not race. Look at Galatians 6:16, First Peter 2:9-10, Romans 4:13; 9:6-8.

"This passage in Genesis 12 has been used by some to intimidate those who do not hold to Zionist views. It's a good promise and is still in affect to the people of God; that is, the new covenant people made up of Jews and gentiles who have placed their faith in Jesus as the only hope of Israel. God is not a respecter of persons and does not give special favor to races of people apart from faith. Our foreign policy as well as our individual attitudes must see Israel as a nation deserving support or censure depending on its actions related to the eternal justice of the Kingdom of God.

"One other note," Uncle Herm continued. "Some will point out that there are several prophecies in the Old Testament predicting a restoration of Israel. First, I think you'll find that none of these promises are to an unbelieving nation.

"Secondly, all those promises are fulfilled in the 'Israel of God' made up of new covenant believers. Jesus was more than even the prophets expected. He more than fulfilled their expectations. The hope of restoration was super-abundantly fulfilled with the resurrection from the dead and the reconstituted people of God. This new people didn't need a temple, for they were themselves the vessels in whom God dwells. They didn't need a restored sacrifice because the final sacrifice had been accepted by God. They didn't need a new city, for they were the salt and light of the world. They didn't need the return to Torah for they now had the word of God written in their hearts. They didn't need a new political entity; they were citizens of the Kingdom of God that had its source in Heaven and its expression on earth. They were no longer limited to a small piece of real estate on the shores of the Mediterranean Sea. They had been commissioned to subdue the earth with the power of *agape*. Look at Hebrews 8:7-13."

"Are you talking about replacement theology?" Paul asked suspiciously.

"And what exactly is that?" Francis sighed, cocking her eyes at Paul. "Remember, all of us don't know these theological terms."

"Replacement theology is another unfortunate term used to label those who don't believe in Israel's literal restoration as the center of God's activity on earth," Uncle Herm explained. "The accusation infers that the objector does not value the place of Israel in God's plan. That is far from truth. Israel has played a major part in God's plan. Remember His original plan was to magnify His Son. Israel was the means of bringing the Son to the world. We owe a lot to Israel's role in history.

"But nothing has been replaced. God has *always* been working through His people of faith. Abraham was a faith person. He was shown the big picture of God's eternal purpose. The Scriptures record that he was looking for a city that was far beyond the physical city of Jerusalem even in its heyday. God's plan didn't involve two peoples. He doesn't have a primary and secondary people. In his letter to the Galatian Christians, Paul made it very clear that the promise made by God to Abraham was to the singular 'Seed' which was Jesus Christ. You can read it in Galatians 3:15-18. Abraham's Seed would bless the nations of the world. Jesus certainly did that and continues to do that through His present Body-temple—the Church.

"The very word *replacement* connotes the idea that God has abandoned His Old Testament people and inserted another people totally different. *Fulfillment* would be a better term. God has fulfilled all His purposes that were predicted and promised in the Old Testament by sending His own Son as the ultimate Israelite who broke down the walls that divided God and man, as well as those that divided Jew and gentile. Jesus fulfilled the purposes of Israel and called His new creation out of both camps. Nothing has been replaced. All things have been made new, as we read in Second Corinthians 5:17."

"But what about the promise to Abraham about the land?" Paul insisted. "Can we talk more about that? Are you *sure* that God doesn't have to give the land to Israel in order to keep His promise?"

Uncle Herm shook his head. "God's promise to Abraham was so much bigger than real estate. He promised to make Abraham a blessing to the whole world. He chose to do that by working through some of the natural descendants of Abraham to produce a singular 'Seed' that would be a blessing to the whole world." Uncle Herm paused, then smiled. "But maybe that's a conversation for another day."

Uncle Herm's Homework

1. Read Appendix A.

2. Discuss how Jesus fulfills the role of Israel.

3. For further reading: a) *Knowing Jesus Through the Old Testament* by Christopher J.H. Wright (Intervarsity Press); b) *Israel in Prophecy* by Phillip Mauro.

CHAPTER 7

Is This a New Gospel?

The sun was still shining a week later when the Armageddon Discussion met again, but now it was too chilly to sit outside. As the group gathered around the fireplace at Uncle Herm's, there was a new energy growing as they discussed these issues. Some old paradigms were being challenged, and discomfort mixed with eagerness to know truth was creating both tension and excitement.

Again, Paul was eager to go first. "Uncle Herm, I'm sorry but I'm having trouble buying this stuff. Where did you get this new way of looking at things? I really believe in the validity of historic creeds and the value of the church that has preceded us. The apostle Paul warned against preaching a new gospel. He said in Galatians 1:8-9 that anyone who did that would be cursed. Where are you getting this new teaching?"

"That's a very valid question," Uncle Herm agreed. "We should never be so presumptuous as to think that God is telling us something brand new. If someone else hasn't heard it, it would be real smart to check out the 'revelation.' On the other hand, our knowledge of history is pretty shallow. We tend to think that 100 years is ancient history. What our branch of the church has accepted as truth for the last 100 years is only a drop in the bucket of our historic faith. It's always the responsibility of every generation to measure the popular teaching of the time to the 'once and for all' faith delivered to the saints. In other words, no creed or popular teaching is to replace the original truths given to us in the Scriptures. As we appreciate the fruit of other generations' struggles with defining truth, we must judge their conclusions as well as ours. I would say that they probably paid more for their understanding than we have any idea, and we should value them more than the 'bubble gum' theology that's popular to a consumer society looking only for a quick fix. Pre-millennial dispensationalism, as presented in the Scofield Bible, is only about 150 years old."

"Okay, I know you want us to think for ourselves, but this is too big," Francis pleaded. "Help us. Where do we start? How are we to take all the writings of all those who have preceded us and then judge them according to the Scriptures when we don't even know for sure how to interpret them ourselves?"

Uncle Herm smiled at Francis. "Okay, let's begin with an effort to understand the gospel as the New Testament writers sought to proclaim it. We've already determined that the 'Kingdom of God' is a theme of the New Testament. The Jewish people were looking for the establishment of this majestic reign of God who would sit in the temple of Jerusalem and rule the nations. Israel would be the superior nation because they were the true people of God.

"When Jesus came declaring that the Kingdom of God was here now, it caused great consternation. They weren't expecting a country-boy messiah who would come into town riding a donkey. Almost immediately the Jewish leaders squared off against Him. Much of the text of the four Gospels is about the conflict between Jesus and those who professed to know His Father. The Jewish leaders were clueless right up through the crucifixion, even being the deciding factor in Jesus' death. After the resurrection and the ascension, Jesus' disciples waited for the empowering of the Holy Spirit which He had promised in John chapters 13 through 17. This happened at the appointed time at Pentecost. It was an expression of the Kingdom of God exhibited in the lives of those believers there. It was truth in practice, not just in theory. It's here that we have the first gospel message proclaimed by the apostles. Peter stood and explained what was happening. He referred to the promises of Old Testament prophets, especially Joel.

"Joel had talked about the last days and what would happen then. Peter said emphatically that Joel's prophecy had come to pass at Pentecost. He explained how the Jewish leaders had totally missed the true interpretation of this prophecy and therefore missed the recognition of Jesus who was also the son of David. This meant that the one they had crucified was the 'King' of the Kingdom for which they had longed.

"The promise that the Old Testament prophets had foretold also included power. The Jewish leaders interpreted that as military and political power. Peter was saying that the promised power is the presence of the Holy Spirit who has come now to live in the believers and do the mighty works of God through them.

"This was radical! The common people heard it and wanted in. But the same spirit that had failed to recognize Jesus was still controlling those who had vested interests in the religious system of the Jews. Three thousand were saved that first day and many were added soon afterward, but the battle continued with the Jewish leaders.

"Enemies help us define what we really believe. This was true of the disciples of Jesus. Because those trying to prove them cultic were confronting them, they reduced their preaching to the basic truths that cannot be denied if one is to be true to Jesus. We call this preaching the 'kerygma.' Peter laid the groundwork for this kind of preaching at Pentecost, but it was carried on by Paul and the other spokesmen recorded in the New Testament. Consider Philip in Acts 8:12-25; Stephen in Acts 7:1-53; Peter in

Acts 10:34-43; Paul in Acts 13:16-52; Acts 24:10-21; Acts 26:1-29; Acts 28:17-20; and First Corinthians 15:3-11.

"The kerygma included some common themes. First, there is continuity between the Old and New Testaments. There are not two gods, one wrathful and strict and another merciful and kind. There are not two separate people of God. God does not have one plan for Jews that is about land and law, and another plan for Christians that is about Heaven and spirit. God has been guiding history from the first. It is all about glorifying His Son. Everything the prophets foretold about the climax of history is about Jesus. If Jesus doesn't fulfill the prophecy, we speculate when we try to find the fulfillment.

"Second, Jesus is the Son of David. He fulfills the expectation of a kingdom. There will not be another kingdom that conforms to the expectations of the earthbound Jewish leaders. Jesus sits on the throne of David *now*.

"Third, Jesus died for the sins of His people of faith. There is no need for further sacrifice of any animal or person. He fulfilled the holy requirements of the law and offers forgiveness to those who believe in Him alone as the atonement for sin.

"Fourth, Jesus was raised from the dead according to the promises of the Scriptures. What had often been interpreted as a mere restoration of land boundaries, rebuilt walls, and temples, was fulfilled in something much greater—the resurrection of the stricken Savior. Think about that. The implications of this are huge! If our Savior is raised, then the life He offers is the resurrected life. The same Spirit that raised Him from the dead is now inside those who believe.

"Lastly, judgment has come already. When Jesus stepped onto the scene, the plumb line of God's eternal justice was established. Those who recognized Him revealed a heart of meekness, while those who didn't revealed a heart of rebellion. All the decisions about rejection and acceptance with God are determined by response to Jesus. Whatever the nature of future judgments, they all will be about what one did with Jesus, the full revelation of God."

"That's great!" Kristy exclaimed. "I don't think I've ever put it all together quite that way. But you said that it was radical. Why? It seems pretty logical to me."

Uncle Herm beamed. "It was, and *is*, radical, Kristy, because what happened was not what they expected. For centuries they had looked for the promises of God to be fulfilled in terms of land, buildings, law, armies, and economy. When Jesus came declaring that He was the fulfillment of the promises, they rejected Him and continued to look for what they wanted.

"And it's still pretty radical. People today have a hard time accepting the present reality of God's Kingdom. It implies a lot of responsibility if we believe we've been given the stewardship of Jesus' inheritance. It seems that we would rather wait for some other epoch of time and hope for Jesus to return to do what *we* were assigned to do."

"Well, that puts a little more meat to the story than I was told when I was presented the gospel," said Paul. "I had the 'Roman Road' read to me. Later I used the 'four spiritual laws' as a way of presenting the gospel message. Do you have to tell all that stuff you just told us in order to preach the gospel?"

"Those evangelistic tools aren't necessarily bad, but we should never forget that the gospel is a story," answered Uncle Herm. "Actually, it is *the* story. The primary problem today, especially with those tracts, is that too often we reduce the gospel to what one has to *do* in order to become a Christian. The focus is on the steps of repentance and the necessary obedience. And we often ask people to make a commitment to Jesus after we have told *our* story. Our testimony and the gospel are related but not the same. Sometimes people try to copy the

77

way we met Jesus rather than respond to the fabulous message of grace that comes in hearing the real story.

"We don't always need to *tell* the whole story, but we should always *know* the whole story. You might remember in Acts 17 that Paul the apostle was preaching to a crowd of philosophers, at Mars Hill, who were not Jewish in their thinking. He told the story of God's eternal meta-narrative in a way they would understand. It was a bit different in presentation than when he spoke to the Jewish crowds, but it contained the basic elements.

"Each of the elements I previously mentioned has enormous implications. We could spend hours mining the gold in each one of those aspects of the kerygma. The gospel is not just a story told to entertain the listeners. Because it's true, it requires tremendous change for those who embrace it. We often make the mistake of thinking that because we have heard it and know the story, we have embraced the truth. That is deception. To have the gospel and not live it is the same mistake the Jews made in having the law but not following it."

"You know, the thing that strikes me is that the preaching of the gospel in the New Testament era was exciting and earth-shattering," Francis reflected. "Today it's boring, mostly. I mean, most of my friends see the gospel as rather old-fashioned and 'doctrinal'... just *boring*."

"Yeah, we need some persecution," Chuck added emphatically. "The Church always does better in persecution. As the end comes, things will get worse and *then* things will get exciting." Chuck was practically rubbing his hands together in anticipation.

Uncle Herm leaned forward in his chair. "You know, Chuck, I've heard that all my life. But I wonder! Why would we wait for things to get worse? Who said it was inevitable that darkness would win? What is the value of the victory that Christ won for us at the cross and the tomb? There's enough darkness in the earth right now for all the excitement we need if we get out of the defeated mind-set of a looming disaster. There is victory now to be appropriated. It affects the whole earth. It's not just about getting people to Heaven. It's about getting the present Kingdom of God implemented on earth. Life is never too exciting while hiding in a bunker. Our Champion has routed the enemy. We are assigned to spoil the enemy's goods while enjoying the victory and exalting our King."

Chuck was stinging a little from the mild rebuke. "Can we talk some more about the Jews and Jesus? I mean, isn't there a special place for ethnic Israel?"

"Okay, Chuck." Uncle Herm smiled at him. "But this is an issue that has caused a lot of division in the church. We're out of time for today, so why don't we address this next time? That will also give you all a chance to do a little homework."

Uncle Herm's Homework

Before our next discussion,

1. Read Galatians, focusing on chapters 3 and 4.

2. Who are the people of God?

3. How do believers in Jesus relate to natural Israel?

4. What is the meaning of the allegory that Paul explains? (See Galatians 4:21-31.)

5. Also read Romans chapters 9–11.

6. Why did Paul write this passage?

7. How many ways is the word "Israel" used?

8. How is salvation offered?

9. What does "hardness" imply?

10. Who are the people of God according to this passage?

CHAPTER 8

Who Are the People of God?

As the group gathered and hung up their coats, there was some discussion about the homework and the possible interpretations of the passages. They were beginning to discover the effort it took to understand Scripture without reading preconceived ideas into it. Meeting with Uncle Herm was awakening a bigger challenge each week.

This week, Uncle Herm was ready with a question. "So, someone tell me why Paul wrote the section of Scripture we find in Romans chapters 9–11."

"He was dealing with the issue of what will happen to the natural Israelites," offered Kristy.

"True," agreed Uncle Herm, "but why does he need to deal with that question at this juncture of his letter to the church at Rome?"

"There were some Jews and some gentiles in the church in Rome and he wanted to explain how God was dealing with each," explained Paul.

"You told us to try to interpret in context, and the context suggests that Paul is answering a possible objection from someone who might raise the question," added Kristy.

"Very good," Uncle Herm nodded. "Paul is writing a letter to the church at Rome. It's a church he has never seen. He didn't plant it and he wants them to know why he is committed to the preaching of the gospel. He may even want the church there to become a home base for his evangelistic work to that portion of the world. In any case, he is very thorough in his spelling out the gospel and its implications to everyone.

"He has made his case that the gospel is no afterthought. The gentiles need it because they have rejected the revelation from nature and have gone on to create gods out of their own imaginations. The Jews need it because they have believed that their connection with God is through natural bloodlines and their possession of the oracles of God. Neither gentile nor Jew has found righteousness apart from grace. It was the God of grace who put all people on the same grounds of neediness and then did for them what they could never do for themselves. He sent His own Son to fulfill the role of the original Adam. Think about what that really means. He started a new race by His death on the cross and the resurrection that followed. This new race was made up of those who came into Christ Jesus by faith alone.

"The law that defined the people of God in the Old Testament was fulfilled by the Spirit living in the people of God in the New Testament. Paul outdoes himself in chapter 8 in his explanation of the life made possible by the life in the Spirit. He makes the point that God's purpose is guaranteed to be accomplished. Nothing can stop what God has planned in summing up the whole of creation in His Son. You can mix all the choices of man together and add the schemes of the devil, but God will get His purpose done. He will have His people, under His rule, blessing the world. He is so adamant that 'all things work together' in Romans 8:28-29 that He is sure some silent objector will ask: 'If God is so good at getting His purpose done, what about His project with Israel? Wasn't that a failure?' So, he writes to explain why Israel's failure to live up to the law is not failure for His purpose."

"Okay, that helps set the context but there are still some things in these verses that aren't clear," said Paul. "Is he talking about natural Israel or spiritual Israel? I did my homework, but I wasn't sure. It seems like he's saying that even all of Abraham's kids were not children of promise."

Paul paused a moment to reflect before he continued. "I guess that makes sense, though. There was selection all the way through with different kids of the patriarchs being those through whom the promise came. You know, it was Isaac not Ishmael, Jacob not Esau, and Judah not Rueben, and so on. But I think he's saying even more than that. I'm just not sure how to phrase it."

"You're right, Paul," agreed Uncle Herm. "The apostle Paul is saying that though the name 'Israel' has always referred to the people of God, there is a fuller meaning, which is the people of faith regardless of their natural descent. Let's look at Romans 9:6-8:

> *But it is not as though the word of God has failed. For not all who are descended from Israel belong to Israel, and not all are children of Abraham because they are his offspring, but "Through Isaac shall your offspring be named." This means that it is not the children of the flesh who are the children of God, but the children of the promise are counted as offspring.*

"That seems pretty clear, doesn't it? God has been guiding history to this climactic point. He now has a people who are themselves the temple of God being indwelt by the Holy Spirit. They are not limited to geographical boundaries or racial distinctives."

Francis was perplexed. "So the point is that there are *not* two separate people of God? Does the Church replace Israel? You mentioned that before, but I wasn't sure…"

"It's important to know who gets the inheritance," insisted Uncle Herm. "If the Church is a temporary interlude in history while waiting for the real people of God, natural Israel, to get back into the picture, then we have limited hope. If, on the other hand, God has been moving history toward this point all along, and the Church is the final people of God on earth, then we can expect the blessing promised to the children to be ours.

"Actually, the Church does not replace Israel, but fulfills its purpose to be a kingdom of priests. We are disciples of the ultimate King and Priest."

"What do you mean by that?" Francis asked. It wasn't getting any clearer for her yet.

Uncle Herm smiled. "I think if we condensed the teaching of Romans 9 through 11, we would conclude that God's plan was to select the Jews as His people for the purpose of blessing the world. How did He do that? In order for the world to have access to God's blessing rather than living under the curse of Adam's fall, sin had to be exposed and forgiven. God picked Abraham's family to be the people who would be His instrument of getting that done."

"Wait a minute," Kristy interjected. "Only Jesus can do that. How does the nation of Israel accomplish that?"

"That's the point!" Uncle Herm was pleased. "Israel fulfilled its role by producing a Messiah who was the ultimate Israelite. After Israel had proven that man is so depraved that he cannot live by law—which was a necessary revelation—it then provided the solution to man's dilemma. Jesus, along with representing all mankind, represented Israel as the sacrifice that

84

satisfied the righteousness of God. That's why Paul can say this in Romans 11:11-12:

> *So I ask, did they stumble in order that they might fall?*
> *By no means! Rather through their trespass salvation*
> *has come to the Gentiles, so as to make Israel jealous.*
> *Now if their trespass means riches for the world, and if*
> *their failure means riches for the Gentiles, how much*
> *more will their full inclusion mean!*

"Israel has played a major role in the drama of redemption. One of Paul's major points is that her fall was in the plan. Failure to live by law had to be proven to man before salvation by grace would be appreciated."

Chuck was confused. "So there's no future for natural Israel in Scripture?"

"Israel's hope is the same as everyone's hope," Uncle Herm reassured him. "Jesus is the goal of history. The only way to relate to God is through His Son. Paul's desire was that the life of the resurrected Christ would be so enticing that Jewish people would want to abandon their shadow-filled religion for the substance-filled life in the new creation."

"Do you think there is some future ingathering of Jewish people into the Kingdom of God?" asked Paul.

Uncle Herm answered slowly and deliberately. "I certainly hope so; I hope there's a future ingathering of all peoples into the Kingdom of God. Equally committed believers have debated this based on their interpretations of Romans 11:25-32. Paul certainly leaves hope for that, but he gives no indication that anyone will ever have a right relationship with God apart from faith in the already revealed Jesus. Look at Romans 11:15: 'For if their rejection means the reconciliation of the world, what will their acceptance mean but life from the dead?'

" 'Life from the dead' is a concept of a returned prodigal. For instance, when Jesus told the story of the prodigal son in Luke 15, the son was said to have been dead and now is alive again. The offer of grace is still open to the prodigal sons of Israel who will accept God's mercy offered in Jesus. When they return, there will be major rejoicing!"

"So tell me again—*why* is all this important?" Francis asked.

"Identifying the people of God who receive the fulfillment of God's promises is very important," explained Uncle Herm. "If natural Israel is the ultimate people of God, we as the Church can't really enjoy the true inheritance left to the Son. If Jesus is not the final fulfillment of God's promise, then we are waiting for the table to be set. If He is, we must come to the table and partake."

"It almost sounds like some Christians think there are two ways of salvation," Kristy said hesitantly.

Uncle Herm nodded his head. "There are those who believe that Jewish people who are practicing Judaism are safe. That would imply that evangelizing Jewish people is unnecessary. They would contend that the Jews have their covenant with God and don't need to be bothered. There are currently some popular preachers on record for those beliefs.

"They do not promote evangelism to Jewish people because they believe that the Jews already have a covenant with God. They have a relationship to God through the law of God as given through Moses.

"I believe this thinking is wrong...and even cruel. Paul the apostle wanted to do all he could so that even some of the Jews would be saved. Look at Romans 11:14. I think it's cruel to withhold the truth from any segment of people. To me that would seem to have the same fruit as 'anti-Semitism.'

"Now, not everyone who considers themselves 'dispensational' would agree with that extreme position. But there seems to be a lot of unnecessary confusion about the identity of the people of God and what the gospel of the New Testament really is."

"That just opens up another whole different area of questions," Francis wailed. "Like, if Jesus is the only way of salvation, isn't that too exclusive? Isn't it presumptuous to say that everyone in the whole world has to come to God through Jesus?"

"Actually, we didn't make that decision," Paul answered confidently. "Jesus made it pretty clear that He considered Himself as the only way to God. For example, in John 14:6 Jesus said, 'I am the way, and the truth, and the life. No one comes to the Father except through Me.'

"The issue is not our narrow-mindedness. When we choose to follow Jesus we don't get the privilege of changing His views, just because we don't understand the justice of them. The issue is the validity of Jesus and His claims. He can't be admired as 'one of the greatest teacher-leaders of all time' if He was wrong on how one relates to God."

Kristy still had questions. "I just wonder, though, if that doesn't turn some people off? It sounds so exclusive. I mean, God is so good and merciful. Would He really restrict the way to Him and keep naïve people out?"

"People aren't 'naïve,' Kristy," Chuck responded. "They're rebellious. Everyone has been given the chance to respond to revelation about God. It's not that they don't know. It's that when they knew, they rejected it. Isn't that right, Uncle Herm?"

"Hey, I'm just enjoying the discussion," laughed Uncle Herm. "You're asking the right questions and finding the right answers." He flipped though his Bible. "But if we go back to Paul's letter to the Romans, we'll find some great instruction about the nature of the gospel. Look at Romans 1:18-23:

> *For the wrath of God is revealed from heaven against all ungodliness and unrighteousness of men, who by their unrighteousness suppress the truth. For what can be known about God is plain to them, because God has shown it to them. For His invisible attributes, namely, His eternal power and divine nature, have been clearly perceived, ever since the creation of the world, in the things that have been made. So they are without excuse. For although they knew God, they did not honor Him as God or give thanks to Him, but they became futile in their thinking, and their foolish hearts were darkened. Claiming to be wise, they became fools, and exchanged the glory of the immortal God for images resembling mortal man and birds and animals and reptiles.*

"Remember that Paul is writing to the church in Rome to explain why he has given his life to the gospel. If being a good Jew would have gained him access to God, he was foolish to suffer such persecution at the hand of the Jews while spreading the gospel. He says the whole world needs the gospel of Jesus Christ because all non-Jewish people have rejected the revelation they received in creation, while all Jewish people can never be made acceptable by animal sacrifices and human effort. All people everywhere need the salvation offered in Jesus Christ."

"But if someone was not reared in a culture that talked about Jesus, they wouldn't have much of a chance would they?" Kristy persisted.

"Remember, Kristy, that knowing Jesus is a matter of the heart," Uncle Herm said gently. "In Romans 10:8-9 we read:

> *But what does it say? "The word is near you, in your mouth and in your heart" (that is, the word of faith that we proclaim); because, if you confess with your mouth that Jesus is Lord and believe in your heart that God raised Him from the dead, you will be saved.*

"Also, remember that Jesus didn't come into existence at His birth. He is eternally the Son of God who is full of mercy. The historical facts about Jesus are vitally important, but one doesn't have to be a historical scholar to know the eternally present Son of God."

"But what exactly did Jesus say about Himself in this area?" Francis asked. "I mean, we can't base something this important on just one verse of Scripture, can we?"

"That's a very good question," smiled Uncle Herm. "Where do you want to start?"

Paul smiled back. "You tell us, and we'll do the study."

"Since John's Gospel is the clearest in presenting the conflict between Jesus and the Jewish leaders, why don't we take some key thoughts from it?" Uncle Herm said. "I think a good study would be John chapters 8 through 12. Jesus makes some pretty absolute claims in these passages. I'll even give you a clue. Jesus operates with the understanding that a person's behavior reveals his father. The Jews seek to kill Him because they are from their father the devil. The Jews are deceived because they think their natural link to Abraham guarantees them favor with God. The true sons of Abraham will recognize Jesus as the Seed of

Abraham and Son of God. The fact that some do not recognize Him reveals their hearts of rebellion. When some Jews do receive Him, they reveal hearts of submission to the revelation they already have."

Uncle Herm smiled. "Now I'll let *you* think about it."

Uncle Herm's Homework

1. Read John chapters 8–12.

2. Examine and comment on each of these phrases of Jesus:

    a. "If you knew Me you would know My Father also" (8:19).

    b. "When you have lifted up the Son of Man then you will know that I am He, and that I do nothing on My own authority, but speak just as the Father taught Me" (8:28).

    c. "If you were Abraham's children, you would be doing what Abraham did" (8:39).

    d. "If God were your Father, you would love Me, for I came from God and I am here" (8:42).

    e. "Your father Abraham rejoiced that he would see My day. He saw it and was glad" (8:56).

f. "For judgment I came into this world, that those who do not see may see, and those who see may become blind" (9:39).

g. "But you do not believe because you are not part of My flock" (10:26).

h. "Now is the judgment of this world; now will the ruler of this world be cast out" (12:31).

3. Why did the Jews of Jesus' day reject Him? What were their issues of disagreement?

4. If you had lived then and had interviewed a respected Pharisee in Jerusalem, what do you think he would have told you about Jesus and His teaching on the Kingdom of God?

5. What are the essentials of faith that define the people of God?

6. How many of the following would be considered one of God's redeemed people? Muslim, Jew, Christian, Buddhist, atheist, spiritualist. Why? Which one would be addressing God if he prayed according to his beliefs?

CHAPTER 9

What About the Land?

Chuck was animated as he bounced into the next meeting, paper in hand. "Hey, I've got a paper here by a noted writer saying that God has to restore Israel in order to keep His eternal promise to give Abraham's seed the land He promised. Can we talk about this some more?"

"Yeah, I've been talking to some of my parents' friends and they mentioned that, too," added Kristy. "What happened to the land promise?"

Uncle Herm settled into his favorite chair. "This *is* an important issue to settle," he said agreeably. "If the Scriptures teach that God still has an unfulfilled promise of natural land to His people, we must look for that people and that land. If that promise was fulfilled by Jesus, and if the 'Israel of God' is made up of the new covenant people of faith, then there is no need to look for that future fulfillment."

"So how do we know?" Kristy asked.

"One key to discovering the truth about this is to remember that the New Testament interprets the Old Testament," responded Uncle Herm. "If all we had was the Old Testament version of the story, we would have to conclude that the land promise was still to come. God did promise to Abraham and his seed a portion of land described with finite boundaries. Look at Genesis 17:3-8:

Then Abram fell on his face. And God said to him, "Behold, My covenant is with you, and you shall be the father of a multitude of nations. No longer shall your name be called Abram, but your name shall be Abraham, for I have made you the father of a multitude of nations. I will make you exceedingly fruitful, and I will make you into nations, and kings shall come from you. And I will establish My covenant between Me and you and your offspring after you throughout their generations for an everlasting covenant, to be God to you and to your offspring after you. And I will give to you and to your offspring after you the land of your sojournings, all the land of Canaan, for an everlasting possession, and I will be their God."

"But the New Testament never mentions the issue of land being restored to Israel."

"One of the major points of this paper is that it was an 'everlasting covenant.' Doesn't that mean that it has to last forever? It also implies that it will happen in the future," Chuck insisted.

"*Everlasting* is used many times in the Old Testament to describe things that have been fulfilled by something greater," explained Uncle Herm patiently. "For instance, the Aaronic priesthood was to be an everlasting priesthood. I think readers of the New Testament would agree that Jesus fulfilled that priesthood. We see that in Hebrews 7:11-28.

"Another *everlasting* was the celebration of Passover mentioned in Exodus 12:14. The sabbath was an everlasting in Exodus 31:17. So was circumcision in Genesis 17:13. All of these were ended in the natural when Jesus came to be the ultimate Seed of Abraham and fulfill the ultimate purpose of these types.

"Wouldn't you agree that Jesus offers the greater and final priesthood, the greater and final passover of salvation, the greater and final sabbath rest, and the greater and final sign of covenant in the circumcised heart?

"So *everlasting* must not refer to the prolonging of the types of these realities. Instead, in the language of the letter to the Hebrews, 'the substance fulfills the shadows.' "

Chuck wasn't entirely convinced. "But isn't that a case of 'spiritualizing' the text? Aren't we supposed to interpret literally?"

Uncle Herm shook his head. "When the New Testament writers explain an Old Testament text, it's not a case of our spiritualizing it. They give the fuller and final meaning to it. *Literal* interpretation is not the same as *natural* or *physical* interpretation. It's not necessary to maintain the natural/physical meaning when it was intended by God to ultimately mean something greater.

"Do you remember what John the Baptist's father, Zechariah, said when he prophesied concerning his son and the ministry he would have in introducing the Savior who had been long promised? Look at Luke 1:68-79:

> *Blessed be the Lord God of Israel, for He has visited and redeemed His people and has raised up a horn of salvation for us in the house of His servant David, as He spoke by the mouth of His holy prophets from of old, that we should be saved from our enemies and from the hand of all who hate us; to show the mercy promised to our fathers and to remember His holy covenant, the oath that He swore to our father Abraham, to grant us that we, being delivered from the hand of our enemies, might serve Him without fear, in holiness and righteousness before Him all our days. And you,*

*child, will be called the prophet of the Most High;
for you will go before the Lord to prepare His ways,
to give knowledge of salvation to His people in the
forgiveness of their sins, because of the tender
mercy of our God, whereby the sunrise shall visit us
from on high to give light to those who sit in darkness and in the shadow of death, to guide our feet
into the way of peace.*

"It seems that he understood the significance of the coming of Jesus as the fulfillment of Old Testament promises. The restoration of Israel was fulfilled ultimately by the resurrection of Jesus. The 'new people' of faith produced by Jesus' resurrection fulfills both Israel's restoration and gentile salvation."

"So, we're supposed to interpret the Old Testament promises in light of New Testament revelation," Chuck stated. "But doesn't the New Testament mention the land promise anywhere?"

"The New Testament consistently refers Jews and gentiles back to the cross and Pentecost as the fulfillment of all promises," said Uncle Herm. "Turn to Acts 3:24-26:

*And all the prophets who have spoken, from Samuel
and those who came after him, also proclaimed these
days. You are the sons of the prophets and of the
covenant that God made with your fathers, saying to
Abraham, "And in your offspring shall all the families
of the earth be blessed." God, having raised up His
servant, sent Him to you first, to bless you by turning
every one of you from your wickedness.*

"In Hebrews 11:8-10 there is commentary on Abraham and the land he was promised. It's clear from New Testament revelation that even while Abraham was in the natural land, he was looking for something greater. He found a greater land in the rest and prosperity of the new covenant. Hebrews 11:8-10 tells us about that:

> *By faith Abraham obeyed when he was called to go out to a place that he was to receive as an inheritance. And he went out, not knowing where he was going. By faith he went to live in the land of promise, as in a foreign land, living in tents with Isaac and Jacob, heirs with him of the same promise. For he was looking forward to the city that has foundations, whose designer and builder is God.*

"It seems clear to me that if we accept the New Testament revelation of the promises made to Abraham and his seed, we will easily conclude that the land that represented the place, peace, and provision for God's people is fulfilled in the new covenant people of God whose king is Jesus."

Paul was thoughtful. "So there's no way to view the natural Jews as the future people of God?"

Uncle Herm didn't hesitate. "Paul, it seems very clear to me that New Testament writers understood the coming of Jesus as the ultimate Seed of Abraham, and recognized that the people God always had in mind were people of faith. Jesus broke down the wall that separated Jews and gentiles and made a *new* race. That's in Galatians 3:7-9:

> *Know then that it is those of faith who are the sons of Abraham. And the Scripture, foreseeing that God would justify the Gentiles by faith, preached the gospel beforehand to Abraham, saying, "In you shall all the nations be blessed." So then, those who are of faith are blessed along with Abraham, the man of faith.*

"Now turn over to Galatians 3:14: 'So that in Christ Jesus the blessing of Abraham might come to the Gentiles, so that we might receive the promised Spirit through faith.'

"Look down a little further to Galatians 3:29: 'And if you are Christ's, then you are Abraham's offspring, heirs according to promise.'

"Finally, in Galatians chapter 4, Paul gives the allegory of the genealogy of Abraham. Notice that it's the natural Jew who corresponds to Ishmael and the believer in Jesus who corresponds to Isaac."

"I'm glad I brought this paper today," Chuck exclaimed. "I've never looked at all this before."

Uncle Herm's Homework

1. When was the land promise fulfilled naturally? (Read 1 Kings 4:21,24; 2 Chronicles 9:26.)

2. What does Hebrews 8:13 mean in relation to the land?

3. Compare Psalm 37:11 with Matthew 5:5. Is this significant?

4. How do you think Ephesians 2:14 and 3:6 relate?

5. Does John 4:20-24 relate? How?

6. Is there any scriptural evidence which indicates that God would restore an unbelieving nation?

7. Does the New Testament promise a restored land? Why?

8. If the land promise is a shadow, what is the substance? (Read Hebrews 9:15; Romans 4:13,16; Galatians 3:29.)

CHAPTER 10

Ultimate Conspiracy

Chuck spent several days going through his library of books that spelled out the various end-time conspiracies. He wasn't sure which ones to keep. After all, they had been a source of satisfaction in at least giving some kind of answers to the nagging questions he had about the battle between good and evil. Through the years, they had given him evidence of several candidates for the final Antichrist.

There were several he knew he could throw away—all those in the "outdated'" group. The scenarios they predicted had already been proven false by time. Looking through them was like a walk back in history. The communist scare had produced many predictions of how it all would end. China still held some imaginative possibilities. Now he had to deal with the different predictions coming out because of the new worldwide terrorist threat. And of course he had to decide what to do with the modern myth in the "left behind" theories.

It was like saying good-bye to old friends, but he was convinced now that many ideas he had accepted as true didn't fit biblical fact. He wanted to accept responsibility for doing his own thinking. He was also beginning to realize that these issues were more important than just material for drama, debate, and discussion. How he thought about the future would affect his choices today.

Finally, the group gathered again, anxious to talk conspiracy.

"I think from what you said last time that you don't believe in any of the conspiracy theories that have been promoted in so many circles," Paul began. "I have to say that sometimes they make some sense. I mean…it does seem that there's some evil force behind all the bad things that happen…you know, besides the devil."

"Fear is the default mode of thinking for the fallen mind," Uncle Herm countered. "Unless we have some revelation from God, we will always tend to explain the constant battle between evil and good with fear as the controlling factor. Of course, there *have* been schemes concocted by depraved minds in history. But the overall scheme as depicted in Scripture does not leave us as victims. God is the ultimate conspiracist."

"What do you mean?" Chuck was a little shocked.

"History is the outworking of God's plan," Uncle Herm explained. "It's under His control. He is so sovereign that He can guarantee the proposed end while giving man the freedom to make choices with real consequences."

There was a long silence as everyone pondered that last statement. Finally, Francis threw up her hands. "All right, fine, I don't get it. How does He do that?"

"I can't explain that one," Uncle Herm admitted. "Who can know the mind of infinite wisdom? We can only know what He reveals to us. When we come to the end of our understanding, we have found a good place to kneel and worship. Read Romans 11:33-36:

> *Oh, the depth of the riches and wisdom and knowledge of God! How unsearchable are His judgments and how inscrutable His ways! For who has known the mind of the Lord, or who has been His counselor? Or who has given a gift to*

Him that he might be repaid? For from Him and
through Him and to Him are all things. To Him be
glory forever. Amen.

Paul was deep in thought. "You said God was a conspir-acist. Can we get back to that?"

Uncle Herm smiled. "Well, that's really not a good word to describe Him. But He does have mystery that only He can explain. And that mystery will explain history when we finally see it."

"What is it?" Francis wanted to know.

"It's the same thing as the gospel that the apostles preached. We spoke of it a little when we talked about the nature of the gospel and the 'meta-narrative,'" said Uncle Herm.

"I've always been taught that when the Bible talks about a mystery, it's speaking of something that was hidden but now is revealed," added Kristy. "It's not what we normally think of as mystery…you know, something that we're still trying to figure out. Is that right?"

"Yes, that's right, Kristy," smiled Uncle Herm. "It's some-thing that mankind would never have figured out apart from God's gracious revelation. Notice that Paul the apostle says in Ephesians 3:3 that he knew the real story only by revelation: 'How the mystery was made known to me by revelation, as I have written briefly.'"

"In a good mystery, you usually know the ending, but don't know how or why it happened that way. God's mys-tery is the ultimate mystery. We know that Jesus came, but we aren't sure of all the reasons until God Himself explains it."

"Go over it again," Chuck insisted. "How does God explain history?"

"At the risk of sermonizing, I'll try to summarize what Paul said in Ephesians chapters 2–3." Uncle Herm paused for a moment, gathering his thoughts.

"When God made man in His image, He was sharing with man the privilege of knowing God and working with God in the earth to express the full glory of God. When man sinned, God spelled out the consequences. That's in Genesis 3:14-15:

> *The Lord God said to the serpent, "Because you have done this, cursed are you above all livestock and above all beasts of the field; on your belly you shall go, and dust you shall eat all the days of your life. I will put enmity between you and the woman, and between your offspring and her offspring; he shall bruise your head, and you shall bruise his heel."*

"In this declaration, God gives the pith of His whole story. The rest of the Bible relates the working out of the conflict between the offspring of the woman and the serpent. God's perfect creation has now been infected with the problem of sin and corruption. His plan for blessing seems to have been thwarted, but God has a plan to fulfill His purpose. He calls a man named Abram who lives in Ur. Turn to Genesis 12:1-3:

> *Now the Lord said to Abram, "Go from your country and your kindred and your father's house to the land that I will show you. And I will make of you a great nation, and I will bless you and make your name great, so that you will be a blessing. I will bless those who bless you, and him who dishonors you I will curse, and in you all the families of the earth shall be blessed."*

"This covenant that God makes with Abram reveals His intention for the rest of the mystery. God will take for Himself a man who will be the father of a people. From this people will come an offspring, a 'Seed,' who will deal with the problem of sin in creation. The whole arrangement between God and Abram is predicated on faith. Abram trusts God to fulfill His promise to bless the nations of the earth through him.

"Actually, though, there are two mandates in that promise. First, there's a 'missionary' mandate that Abram's Seed will bless all nations, not just his own. Then there is the 'messianic' mandate, which is the means that God will use to fulfill the promise. God gave the law to Moses to give to the messianic people. Though they could not live up to its holy requirements, they produced the ultimate Israelite: Jesus, who not only lived up to the requirements but also fulfilled the law by paying the penalty of those who had transgressed it. Those who by faith entered into relationship with Jesus are the Israel of God who will bless all nations by proclaiming the gospel to them."

"Did the Old Testament saints know this?" Chuck asked.

Uncle Herm shook his head. "They didn't fully understand the story. Only after the coming of Christ did the Holy Spirit reveal the full story. Look at First Peter 1:10-12:

> *Concerning this salvation, the prophets who prophesied about the grace that was to be yours searched and inquired carefully, inquiring what person or time the Spirit of Christ in them was indicating when he predicted the sufferings of Christ and the subsequent glories. It was revealed to them that they were serving not themselves but you, in the things that have now been announced to you through those who preached the good news to you by the Holy Spirit sent from heaven, things into which angels long to look.*

"None of the prophets or saints of the Old Testament could have imagined the amazing and surprising way God would finally keep His promises to Abraham and His people.

The insight is only available by the revelation of the Holy Spirit. By the perspective of that revelation, we can see that the Old Testament was the buildup, the New Testament the climax, and we live now in the epilogue of the story. Those without revelation are still trying to figure it out."

"In Ephesians, Paul says that the mystery is that the gentiles are included in the household of God. Is that what you're saying?" Francis wanted to know.

"Yes," Uncle Herm agreed. "That includes a lot. Notice the heart of the gospel in Paul's own words in Ephesians 3:7-12:

> *Of this gospel I was made a minister according to the gift of God's grace, which was given me by the working of His power. To me, though I am the very least of all the saints, this grace was given, to preach to the Gentiles the unsearchable riches of Christ, and to bring to light for everyone what is the plan of the mystery hidden for ages in God who created all things, so that through the church the manifold wisdom of God might now be made known to the rulers and authorities in the heavenly places. This was according to the eternal purpose that He has realized in Christ Jesus our Lord, in whom we have boldness and access with confidence through our faith in Him.*

"The law that God had given to Israel had become a wall that divided people. Through the cross and resurrection, that wall was destroyed. Now all people of all races have open access to God. This is what astounds the powers that are behind the evil schemes of history. They never figured that God would destroy hostility like this. These powers traffic in hostility and division. The cross of Christ cuts at the root of all divisiveness and hostility. It makes it possible for all peoples, both sexes, all social classes to come to God the same way and know Him fully. The division between gentile and

Jew was once ordained by God and served its purpose, but it's now obliterated."

"The powers of hell didn't know this?" Kristy was incredulous.

"No. This perspective comes only by revelation to those whose hearts are open to God," said Uncle Herm. "But you can be sure that satan hates the Church. It reminds him of the ultimate defeat of his hostility. The Church as defined by Scripture is the answer to the divisiveness and hostility that marks fallen mankind. It is the people of God who relate to Him by faith and have the privilege of blessing the whole world."

"So that's why there's such a battle against the Church!" Chuck was amazed. "If people ever saw the true story, they would run to be a part of the people of God who are united in their worship of Him. I guess that helps answer the question of why there's so much division even in the ranks of Christ's followers. Satan is still trying to promote division and hostility."

"Exactly!" Uncle Herm was pleased with Chuck's analysis. "The confusion over the identity of the people of God is a distraction coming from the deceiver. The defensiveness of those who promote their brand of religion is also part of the deceiver's work. The powers of evil hate the Church and seek to diffuse it any way possible. Since the final Seed of woman has defeated the devil, the only weapons he has are deception and distraction. The Church is where God's peace reigns, where sins are removed, and distinctions are not divisions. It is certainly not 'Plan B' in God's purposes. It's the only way God planned to fulfill His promise to Abram that his Seed would bless the whole world. Flip over to Ephesians 3:20-21:

> *Now to Him who is able to do far more abundantly*
> *than all that we ask or think, according to the power*

at work within us, to Him be glory in the church and in Christ Jesus throughout all generations, forever and ever. Amen.

"Wow! I think I see why there's been such a battle regarding the Church. It's more important than I realized." Francis thought for a moment. "I think I should be a little more reluctant to criticize the Church. It's made up of imperfect people but it's also God work." She sighed. "I just wish it weren't so divided. Why can't we just have church the way they did in the New Testament?"

"I'm beginning to see that some of the problem with the Church is the failure to recognize the magnitude of what happened at the coming of Jesus," Paul stated. "We've been acting more like Old Testament saints than New Testament ones. The believers of the New Testament were so excited about this new life and its potential they were willing to sell out for it. We've reduced it to some principles to live by while we wait for God to do something else. I want to regain the passion they had. I think I'm beginning to see that my perspective must change before the passion comes."

Uncle Herm agreed. "Someone famous once said that the gospel has not failed in the world. It just hasn't been tried. The mystery as explained by Paul should motivate us to believe passionately and behave passionately. God has provided everything we need to live as victors on this earth. He has forgiven our sins, made our bodies His temple, and placed us into a community of faith with each person being gifted to get the job done. With a healthy relationship to Him as head and the Church as members, we can finally do what Adam was commissioned to do."

Francis still had questions. "You said that we could live with distinctives not being divisive. So everyone doesn't have to do it the same way, right? I mean, people with other cultures don't have to necessarily give up their culture to become a Christian, do they?"

"One of the mistakes we make in our missionary work is transferring our American culture rather than the gospel to other countries." Uncle Herm leaned forward in his chair. "Actually, the Kingdom of God has its own culture. All cultures have to bow to that. Where our culture does not contradict the Kingdom culture, it can carry on. God likes differences and distinctives. It's where our values violate those of God's Kingdom that we get into trouble. We either try to 'baptize' our cultural idols or we react against the differences and demand that everyone accept uniformity."

"So how would you advise us to distinguish which cultural practices are compatible with the Kingdom of God?" Paul asked.

"A couple of issues must be constant," explained Uncle Herm. "First, Jesus is the final and full revelation of God. Second, love is the supreme evidence of faith in God. When these are fully accepted, culture will conform to the values of God's Kingdom. But when Jesus plus 'something else' is the issue and word games are played with 'love,' that means trouble is up. When these are not real in a community, other practices become major. Dress, various laws and requirements, external expressions of holiness, and judgmentalism become dominant in the atmosphere. Everyone wants to feel special. If we in our carnality find ways that we can feel superior to others because of our supposed special relationship with God, we tend to magnify that practice that sets us apart."

"I don't know when I have been so confident in the gospel of Jesus Christ!" Kristy exclaimed. "The study you've prompted us to do has made me aware of the power of the gospel. It's really worth giving your life for. I have hope that

I can have a passion similar to the believers in the Book of Acts. I'm seeing a glimpse of something more wonderful than I've ever seen. Sharing the powerful life of Jesus *now*...that's something!"

Paul turned to Uncle Herm. "Would you take just a minute and summarize what we said here?"

"Everyone wants answers to the big questions," Uncle Herm began. "Why are we here? Why is there evil in God's world if He is good? What is the Bible about? Is there a purpose for everything, even me? Every culture tries to answer these questions. Without the aid of God's wisdom, no one will ever correctly find the answers. So conspiracy theories abound. Since the fallen mind operates in the fear mode, the schemes that seem to give some answers are filled with ingeniously wicked strategies. We are usually left as victims of those much smarter and with more resources. The devil gets a lot of publicity as we try to survive. Our hope is usually reduced to a day in the shadowy future when our God will in the nick of time rescue us.

"But God's story of history is not about our victimization. It is about His purposes and our liberation. He has always planned to glorify His Son. His creation was for that purpose. We were made to enjoy God like He enjoys Himself. We were given the privilege of working with God in glorifying Him in the earth. When our forefather sinned, God began the process of glorifying His Son by preparing a people who would produce the ultimate Seed that would solve the problem of sin for all peoples of the earth. Jesus is that Seed. He has come to deliver all who come to God by faith in Him. Through this people, God will continue to glorify His Son by their demonstrating His life in their own. They can still subdue the earth and demonstrate the Kingdom of God on earth. They have experienced the power of reconciliation. Now they are instruments of that power.

"The forces of evil work through division and hostility. God's people, the Church, are the ones who can defeat division and hostility. They are one with God and with each other. As they recognize their already accomplished unity of Spirit, they will walk toward the possible unity of faith. They are already victors, because they embody the very life of Christ in the person of the Holy Spirit. They fulfill every shadow and type of God's people in the Old Testament. They are His by redemption. They are under His rule of agape-love, and they are His living temple. The mystery is explained."

Uncle Herm's Homework

1. Define *mystery* as the word is used in the New Testament.

2. Describe the nature and purpose of "Church" from Ephesians chapters 2 and 3.

3. What was the mystery that was hidden in the Old Testament?

4. Compare Paul's concept of "Church" with the common perception today. (List the comments you have heard by you and others regarding the Church.)

5. Now read Ephesians 4. What should be our focus today?

6. In one hundred words explain the mystery.

CHAPTER 11

The Crash of Spaceship Earth

"Christians aren't the only pessimistic ones," Kristy stated at the next group meeting. The wind outside was howling around Uncle Herm's house as the young people gathered inside. Kristy had been working up for this all week and couldn't wait to get started.

"I've been noticing that there are a lot of people who aren't very optimistic, yet they don't buy into any biblical explanation of reality, either," she continued. "What I mean is, it's not a matter of biblical interpretation for them. Instead, they quote scientists and environmentalists who predict a dismal future based on the earth's limited resources and the specter of over-population."

"That's true," Francis agreed. "I have friends who don't know anything about biblical eschatology yet they seem to lack purpose and passion too. They're convinced that there are no meaningful choices. Their motto is essentially: 'In the end we're all dead.' "

"But they are affected by biblical or unbiblical beliefs, because the Church is the salt of the earth and the light of the world," Paul insisted. "When the Church is defective, the whole world is harmed, even if unconsciously."

"Good point," Uncle Herm affirmed. "There's certainly more to our hopeless malaise than arguments about the end of the world. But Paul is right. When we as believers become passive toward our stewardship of the earth, the unbelievers are left with explanations that aren't right. When we don't speak truth into the discussion about earth's problems, the only voices heard are the ones that disregard God. Those voices create speculative answers but no real solutions."

"So, how do we speak into the discussion about 'Spaceship Earth' heading for a crash?" Francis wanted to know.

"We could start with reclaiming some definitions and dispelling some myths," Uncle Herm responded.

Francis looked at him quizzically. "What myths?"

"For one, we could examine the often-used phrase 'limited resources,' " said Uncle Herm. "What is the resource that is limited and where are the limits?"

Chuck jumped into the discussion. "Well, it just stands to reason that we can't keep using up the earth's resources. I mean...like fossil fuels; they're going to run out one day."

Uncle Herm smiled. "I remember an older man telling me what a problem it was for a Texas rancher to have that messy black stuff oozing out of the ground in his back pasture. That was only a few years ago."

Chuck laughed. "That sounds like the *Beverly Hillbillies*. I saw that once on cable. But seriously, are you saying that oil was the solution to an energy problem at the time, and we can expect more of those kinds of discoveries?"

"Well, that *was* quite a discovery and provided a great jump in progress for mankind," Uncle Herm said. "But the solution was at least partially the product of a creative mind. The oil was there all the time and was actually a problem until the creative mind got involved."

"So the resource is *the mind*?" Chuck was startled.

Uncle Herm continued. "A biblical perspective sees the universe as created by a personal God who created it out of nothing and governs it through His people created in His image—people with built-in creativity. A good reference here is Hebrews 11:3."

"What perspective of reality does the world have?" Francis asked.

"In our society the prevalent view would see the world as a closed system with matter being all that exists—no god, no creation, no more resources than we can observe," explained Uncle Herm. "So it's not surprising that the conclusion would be that there is the proverbial limited pie. If you get a bigger piece, I get a smaller one. This would lead to a view of wealth and poverty that demands the rich to redistribute to the poor. The rich have victimized the poor, and the only solution is to enact laws and incite social pressure to take from those who have and redistribute to those who don't have."

"We talked about that in my economics class!" Kristy exclaimed. "One of our assignments was to read *The Population Bomb* by Paul Ehrlich. His premise is that the poor have been victimized." With a questioning look, Kristy turned to their guide. "Uncle Herm, how *should* Christians view wealth and poverty?"

Uncle Herm began to outline the biblical perspective: "The world as we discover it through God's revelation is our stewardship. God who created it from nothing is our resource. He has offered to give us whatever knowledge we need to establish His rule on this earth."

Uncle Herm leaned back in his chair. "Now, what do you think that would look like?"

Everyone paused to think, but Paul was the first to blurt out an answer. "What about...Goodness in charge!"

"I like that." Uncle Herm smiled. "I think the creative, good, purposeful, inexhaustible God working through His obedient people will develop the earth's potential beyond anything we can imagine. There are untold mysteries hidden in the universe that can be explored by people who are hopeful enough to look."

"But isn't it true that the world is getting too many people on it?" Chuck persisted. "Aren't we running out of food?"

Uncle Herm shook his head. "No! The facts don't bear that out. In his book, *Discipling the Nations,* Darrow Miller quotes these statistics: Food supply has more than doubled in the last 40 years, much faster than population growth. Life expectancy has increased in every world region since 1950. And the worldwide child mortality rate has declined from 250/1000 in 1950 to 84/1000 in 1998.[2]

Food prices have actually fallen in the last 50 years in spite of warnings from the closed-system pessimists."

"That's amazing!" Chuck exclaimed. "All I ever hear about is the looming disaster in our future. So, we as a race could be here awhile and maybe even make things better, huh?"

Uncle Herm pulled out his Bible. "Think about what the apostle Paul had in mind when he wrote Romans 8:19-21:

> For the creation waits with eager longing for the revealing of the sons of God. For the creation was subjected to futility, not willingly, but because of Him who subjected it, in hope that the creation itself will be set free from its bondage to decay and obtain the freedom of the glory of the children of God.

"You wonder if maybe we could begin to see some of that as we appropriate the victory that already belongs to the children of God while we wait for the ultimate consummation."

"So, where did this pessimistic view come from?" Francis wanted to know.

"It is the inevitable conclusion of a worldview that believes matter is all that matters," Uncle Herm said slowly. "If what we see is all that exists, and there is no transcendent God outside of creation, then we have reason to be concerned about the future of the world. But if God, who is Creator and not a part of creation, is still alive and active in carrying out a purpose, we can hope in His promises.

"While the Church was fussing about ecclesiology, people like Descartes, Nietzsche, Darwin, Malthus, and Margaret Sanger promoted ideas largely uncontested by biblical thinkers. When we as a culture get tired of the fear and hopelessness coming from these ideas, maybe we'll consider again the truth that sets men free."

"So, the fatalism that is often backed up with Bible verses…is that bad interpretation again?" Kristy wondered.

"It can be," Uncle Herm agreed. "As we discussed before, we tend to read through our 'presuppositional' glasses. For some, the Bible is filled with proof-texts and verses that predict the destruction of the earth—so it's easy to believe the scenarios presented by the secularists.

"Actually, many of the verses used to confirm imminent destruction of the earth are referring to events already past. Old Testament prophecies spoke of God's judgment coming through invading armies. These things happened just as they said. One of the most important was the unmatched destruction of the world of Old Testament Judaism in 70 A.D. There are numerous Scriptures that refer to that particular destruction, which is obviously in our past.

"But the Bible makes it abundantly clear that God is in complete control of creation and can and will conclude history His way. The focus of Scripture is not about the earth's destruction, but its stewardship. God has placed untold mysteries in creation, and has created mankind with creative imaginations that, when liberated by eternal truth, will discover marvelous solutions to earth's problems."

Francis was amazed. "Why haven't we heard this before? I mean, why have we been so focused on other things?"

"I think we've all been confused on the issue of accountability," Uncle Herm said gently. "It's a word that conjures up ideas of limitation. For some, it's a system of sin-management. It's a picture of someone looking over our shoulder checking on every detail. We only ask for it when we have a problem we can't solve alone, like addiction. Actually, it's what gives meaning to our life here. God has given us the dignity of making choices that have consequences and there will be an accounting. We'll all give account of the gifts and graces left in our hands."

"I know that's true," Paul said hesitantly, "but to be honest, that sounds like works instead of grace."

"Okay, here's the difference," Uncle Herm explained. "The sin issue is settled on the basis of faith in Jesus as our atonement. We won't face our sins in the future, but we will face our stewardship."

"What do you mean?" Chuck was puzzled. "I thought I would have to attend the universal gathering of all people who ever lived while the video of my life was played. I've always dreaded that day. All of my sins would be exposed for all to see. Isn't that the 'judgment seat of Christ'?"

"I don't think so, Chuck," said Uncle Herm. "When Jesus takes our sin, we never have to face it again. He has freed us from the preoccupation with sin and given us the privilege of working with Him in stewarding the earth. Now He gives us each an assignment with matching ability and wisdom, and He even gives us Himself. When we do something that fulfills His purposes, He gives us rewards."

Chuck shook his head. "That sounds too good to be true. So how do we view our sin?"

"Sin is missing the mark of our destiny," explained Uncle Herm. "When we acknowledge it as sin, we're given a fresh start without condemnation. Without fear of reprisal, we can give our whole heart to glorifying God through using our stuff to the greatest advantage. A good verse to reference is First John 1:9."

"So our aim should be to use whatever we have for the purposes of expanding the Kingdom of God on earth?" Francis asked rhetorically.

Uncle Herm smiled. "That sounds like a mission statement for the people of God everywhere."

"Does that also mean there are going to be degrees of blessing in Heaven?" Francis continued.

"I don't think there's any question that some will have more rewards than others to lay at the feet of Jesus," agreed Uncle Herm. "So it would be a good strategy to spend the most energy sending most of your stuff to the place you'll spend most of your time. We're going to be on this earth for a relatively short time. We can lay up treasure in Heaven by the choices we make on earth. When we get there, the identity of the rich and poor will be radically different. Look at First Timothy 6:17-19."

Francis nodded her agreement. "I can see that. If we live with eternity in view, it will affect every choice, right?"

"Absolutely!" Uncle Herm was pleased. "We are accountable 24-7 for our choices. Nothing is considered secular. It's all about living the whole life of Christ all the time."

Francis hesitated. "I think I like that, but it seems to make life too serious. Can we take a day off sometimes?"

"It's all a day off." Uncle Herm paused to smile at the perplexed looks on their faces. He continued, "We live in the ultimate sabbath. The work that causes strife has been done. Because we are made in God's image, and because He is a worker, we all long to work. We will always be doing something. God has made it possible for us to work with Him and enjoy the fulfillment of that work."

Francis was flustered. "You know what I mean. If we're accountable for everything...every single dime, how can we enjoy just 'hanging'?"

"Maybe you've forgotten that God likes pleasure, fun, recreation, celebration, and 'hanging'—a good synonym of fellowship," Uncle Herm reminded them. "God commanded the Israelites to have prolonged feasts several times a year. He encouraged them to celebrate excessively. He still wants us to enjoy His creation. He knows, however, that because we have been born of the Spirit, we'll get the most enjoyment out of investing our lives in Kingdom projects. Vacations and yachts are fun for awhile, but the real joy of the believer is in service."

"You're right," Francis said. "It does make a difference when you can believe that your work is not doomed to failure and that your choices really do matter. I'm tempted to believe we could actually make a difference in this world before we die. I'd never really thought about living in fellowship with Someone who can create something out of nothing and raise the dead. That does put a whole new light on things. It would be hard to be hopeless if you really believed that."

---

[2] Darrow L. Miller, *Discipling the Nations* (Seattle, WA: YWAM Publishing, 1998), 161-162.

Uncle Herm's Homework

1. Review the original mandate for mankind in Genesis 1:26-28. What would that look like today?

2. What is your favorite "conspiracy theory"? What Scriptures are used to promote it? Interpret them in context.

3. Why does God *not* want us to be sin conscious?

4. What does stewardship mean to you right now?

5. What kind of rewards do you expect at the final judgment?

CHAPTER 12

Living Today With Passion and Purpose

At the group's next gathering, Uncle Herm was ready to start the discussion. "Last time, we talked a lot about the ideas that created or have fostered the pessimism of our day. Today I'd like to discuss the solution. We have good reasons to live passionately with profound purpose."

"That would be great!" Francis said enthusiastically. "I'd like to have a clear understanding of what we can expect now, and what we're getting in the future. I'm starting to believe we're destined to do something here other than wait for Heaven."

"Yeah, but if you emphasize the present victory too much, you'll be called 'kingdom now' people...whatever that means," Chuck cautioned.

"Well, what we're called by others is not the prime motive for our stance," Uncle Herm admonished gently. "We must come to some understanding of what the Bible teaches us to expect on this earth and not confuse it with what's preserved for us after this life on earth."

"Okay, then what *does* the Bible teach about our state of victory now?" Chuck challenged.

Kristy sighed. "I know you're going to tell us to study for ourselves and become biblical thinkers who don't depend on others to spoon-feed us. But could you *please* just teach us for a while and then let us ask questions? I promise we'll do our study."

"Okay," Uncle Herm grinned sympathetically. "I'll show you a little mercy. Let's take the Gospel of John as an example and see what we can learn from that disciple's account of the life Jesus lived and transferred to us.

"You already know that John wrote one of the four Gospels in the New Testament. His is a little different from the other three, which are called the 'Synoptic Gospels.' One of the features of John's Gospel is his use of the term 'signs.' He chooses a few of the miracles that Jesus performed and shows how each pointed to something about Jesus that fulfilled God's promise to Abraham regarding blessing the whole world."

"Isn't it true that, of all the Gospel writers, John gave the clearest explanation for writing his Gospel?" Paul asked.

"Yes, that's right," Uncle Herm affirmed. "Do you know what it is?"

"It's in chapter 20, verse 31," Paul responded. " 'But these are written so that you may believe that Jesus is the Christ, the Son of God, and that by believing you may have life in His name.' "

"So now we know why John wrote this account," Uncle Herm said. "If we get out of it what he intends, we'll believe that Jesus is the One promised in the Old Testament, and we'll have the life He demonstrated while on earth. I think we'd all settle for the life Jesus lived, wouldn't we?"

"Can we really expect to live like that?" Paul was incredulous.

"As a man rightly related to God, yes!" Uncle Herm stated emphatically. "We can have the same access to the Father as Jesus. We can know our calling as Jesus did. We can live by the power of the Holy Spirit as Jesus did. Are we divine like Jesus? No, but it was not His divinity that allowed Him to live in victory. He lived by faith in the Father. When He died for our sins, He died as God-man. It took the perfect sacrifice to pay the penalty for our sins. He lived by constant fellowship with the Father. We can do the same works He did because He did only what the Father either told Him or showed Him."

"So how did John show that Jesus was the ultimate revelation of all Old Testament promises?" Paul asked. "How do we learn from him how to access this life that Jesus lived?"

Uncle Herm smiled. "John starts off with a familiar sounding refrain: 'In the beginning...' "

"Even *I* recognize that," Francis exclaimed. "Genesis!"

"Right," Uncle Herm continued. "John is saying that the appearance of Jesus in the history of time is as radical as original creation. Jesus started something new. As God spoke in the beginning and created the universe, He has spoken again. This time it's through the Son. Jesus is God's ultimate Word...His thoughts put into expression. The Christ-event is not one of many important events in history. It is *the* event.

"He goes on to say that Jesus came first to His own people, the Jews, but they rejected Him; and He created a new nation of people by giving everyone the authority to become His sons by faith in Him. The remainder of the Book is about Jesus bringing the ultimate revelation of God, but being rejected by those who supposedly knew God.

"Every miracle was a message. For His first miracle, Jesus turned water into wine. Moses had turned the Nile into blood as His first miracle. Jesus is greater than Moses and the exodus now at hand is greater than the one experienced by Israel back then.

"It was at a wedding that the first sign was done. Jesus is the ultimate Bridegroom and the feast is ready. Remember, back then only the bridegroom had the authority to provide the wine. The wine Jesus provides is the Holy Spirit who produces in us the power to live like He did.

"With eyes to see, we understand that Jesus is clearly the point of the whole Bible and the ultimate star of history. The hostility of the unbelieving Jews brought into stark relief the truth regarding the Christ, the Son of God. As they opposed Him, He was able to show the contrast between relationship with God and false religion. Their tests which were designed to catch Him in error only served to reveal their deception. Their questions gave Him the opportunity to answer with final truth. Their total rejection of Him revealed their rebellious hearts and sealed the doom of their system. Read First Thessalonians 2:14-16. In it all, Jesus is revealed as the only One worthy of worship."

"That's really fascinating," Kristy said. "So that's the way to read John?"

"John's purpose dictates how we read," replied Uncle Herm. "John is determined to show how the Old Testament has continuity with the New Testament, and how Jesus is greater than all the types and shadows that pointed to Him."

"Do more!" Kristy encouraged.

"Let's skip over to chapter 5," Uncle Herm said, thumbing the well-worn pages of his Bible. "There's a story of a man who has been coming to the pool of Bethesda for 38 years hoping to finally get into the pool at the right time. As the story goes, he can be healed if he does.

"Let's set the stage for this sign. The pool is close to the sheep gate. That's where the sheep are brought in and examined to see if they qualify to be offered at temple sacrifice. The ones that are defective are culled and placed in a certain pen. The comparison of the 'disqualified' people and the sheep is easy. They're in an area covered with five porches. Ring any Old Testament bells?"

"Are you asking for numerology?" Paul asked. "What the number five stands for?"

"Well, what is the most prominent 'five' in the Old Testament?" Uncle Herm clarified.

"The five Books of the Law?" Francis guessed.

"Right! So the point here is that the people are defective and disqualified and they live under the law. It, like the pool, gives hope that if they were able to perform certain tasks they could receive the promised blessing. But the testimony of the man is that he has been hoping for 38 years and still has no cure. He has good excuses but no healing."

"Boy, that sounds familiar," Paul sighed. "That's the way we live. Maybe I should say, the way I live."

Uncle Herm shrugged. "It's the way of the law. Everyone who lives with the focus on the requirements and qualifications will find himself or herself defective. Anyone who continues to believe he or she is only a little way from victory is doomed to years around the pool. They are always focused on that 'one more step' that will get them to the top."

"So Jesus comes up to the man..." Paul prompted.

"Jesus approaches the man and asks a probing question: 'Do you want to be well?'" Uncle Herm paused. "At first glance, that would seem like an unnecessary question. Sure he wanted to be well. He had been coming for 38 years. But Jesus doesn't ask foolish questions. To get well meant that the man would leave those around the pool. I'm sure he had bonded with the others who were not only sick, but also victims of life. No one would put them into the pool either. But the real clincher was that healing was being offered now! *Now?* He thought. *Are You talking about* **now**...**now**? It's hard to go from hope to faith. When you have lived with the 'someday' mentality, 'today' is hard to believe. Hebrews 3:7-19 is a good reference to read."

"This is getting personal," Kristy said reluctantly. "So part of his problem was the immediacy of the healing?"

"Well, it didn't look like he had anticipated this, and it required a faith that acted now," answered Uncle Herm.

"Notice the nature of the encounter. Jesus gives a command: 'Get up! Pick up your bed and walk.' It's that word from the Word that creates life. When Jesus speaks, something happens. He is the one who created the universe by a word...remember? Now He has invaded the sick room and His word offers a whole new life. When He says 'get up,' nothing in creation except unbelief can stop your getting up."

"I'm amazed!" Kristy interrupted. "I've never seen that! Please, keep going!"

"Well, the man acts on the word of Jesus and gets up," Uncle Herm continues. "He leaves and goes toward the temple. He can walk for the first time in 38 years.

"But there are a few more things to notice here. Jesus' command makes hope turn into faith. When a command is given, you have to act on it or refuse to act on it. In other words, when He speaks we can either obey and see His miracle, or we can disobey. For instance, the Jews were watching the fulfillment of Old Testament prophecies walk in their midst, yet refused to believe it. They were determined to wait until it looked like what they had expected."

Kristy shook her head. "What a shame! They could have experienced the same kind of miracle."

"But did you notice?" Uncle Herm leaned forward. "Jesus didn't come to the pool and announce that healing was now available for everyone because the Messiah had come. It was not a proposition He offered. It was not blanket salvation apart from personal relationship with Jesus. Jesus the person came to the man, a person, and dealt with him on the basis of a personal need and personal faith. It's so much more than believing in the doctrine of redemption or reconciliation. God refuses to save us from hell only. He wants fellowship—partnership."

"Are you referring to some wrong emphasis that is being taught?" Francis asked cautiously.

Uncle Herm smiled. "I know that we all like to reduce things to formulas. If we could figure out a way to have the blessing without having to deal with God Himself, we would. We still have a lingering mentality that God is off somewhere watching and we want to do whatever makes Him favorable toward us. If we're told that faith pleases Him, we'll try to find a way to 'faith.' But the kind of faith that pleases Him is the kind that keeps us in intimate fellowship with Him responding to His words. To believe His words without confronting Him is a shortcut He won't allow.

"But the story is not finished. The man has experienced the 'now' reign of the present Messiah. He goes to the temple, and Jesus finds him there. This time Jesus gives a new command: 'Sin no more!' Jesus is not just interested in the well body. The same word that can heal the body can heal the soul. *You mean I don't have to sin anymore?* the man must have thought. That very thought gives hope, and hope purifies, as we read in First John 3:3."

"Now there's ground for some real hope," Paul added thoughtfully. "I like that. I've been led to think that sin is inevitable. As we look around at friends who are addicted or at ourselves when we can't get victory over certain weaknesses, the thought that Jesus would speak a personal word that would empower us—that's hope!"

Uncle Herm continued. "Forgive me for wanting to finish the story, but it fits so well with what you're saying. Did you notice that Jesus healed this man on the sabbath? This really got the Jews upset. He was dishonoring the sabbath, according to their system. But for the man, sitting around doing nothing— which was sabbath keeping—was not much of a rest. He did that all the time. Real rest was being able to do what he was created to do. That is the sabbath fulfilled. Jesus gives the rest that stops our feverish activity and replaces it with the quiet ability to do what we are designed to do. The Jews had defined it by prohibition. Jesus defined it by productivity. Jesus kept the real sabbath by giving the ultimate rest to one who had struggled with sickness and sin."

"I can see so many parallels," Kristy added, her eyes wide with awe. "What would you say is the most important insight in this account?"

"Hope turning to faith when Jesus speaks is the thing that jumps out at me," Francis interjected. "I'm going to ask Him to speak to me daily. I want to see Him working His life through me. I have hope that He'll speak and when He does, I can act. That would make fellowship with God more than devotional. I want to walk with Him every day. Who knows, He might just tell me to heal the sick, raise the dead..."

"...or just love someone with His kind of love," Kristy finished.

Chuck spoke up. "I've been pretty quiet, but I can tell you, this is awesome. I guess I hadn't really grasped the privilege of living in the 'now.' I've postponed too many blessings to a future when circumstances might be better. I've been living under the five porches even though I'm not an Old Testament Israelite. I constantly think I'll get a victory if I can just get a little better, or try a little harder, pray more, study more, become committed."

"I can see clearer," Paul agreed. "But I still don't know what word of Jesus to act on and what to wait for."

Uncle Herm was thoughtful. "We often idealize the days of Jesus with His disciples. We tend to think they had the advantage because Jesus was physically there. Actually, Jesus said that when He ascended and sent the Holy Spirit, it would be better. Look at John 14:16-18:

> *And I will ask the Father, and He will give you another Helper, to be with you forever, even the Spirit of truth, whom the world cannot receive, because it neither sees Him nor knows Him. You know Him, for He dwells with you and will be in you. I will not leave you as orphans; I will come to you.*

"And again, look at John 16:7:

> *Nevertheless, I tell you the truth: it is to your advantage that I go away, for if I do not go away, the Helper will not come to you. But if I go, I will send Him to you.*

"Look further down that chapter in verses 12 and 13:

> *I still have many things to say to you, but you cannot bear them now. When the Spirit of truth comes, He will guide you into all the truth, for He will not speak on*

131

His own authority, but whatever He hears He will speak, and He will declare to you the things that are to come.

"And again, in verses 23 and 24:

In that day you will ask nothing of Me. Truly, truly, I say to you, whatever you ask of the Father in My name, He will give it to you. Until now you have asked nothing in My name. Ask, and you will receive, that your joy may be full.

"If we are to take Jesus' expectations for those who follow Him after His ascension, we can anticipate an intimate fellowship with the Father just like the one demonstrated by Jesus while on earth. I think we're so fixed on the physical that we miss the reality of the spiritual. We long for Jesus to return physically while He yearns for us to access the privilege of walking in fellowship now.

"Would it be better for us if Jesus came back physically and lived in one locale? He lives as surely today as He did then and better, because He lives in the temple of our bodies. We all have the same access to the Father that Jesus did as a man."

"So is the problem that we just don't believe that?" Paul asked.

"I think that's the heart of the problem," Uncle Herm agreed. "If we don't believe it's possible to have this kind of intimate communication, we certainly won't expect it.

"But there are other factors, too. I don't think we appreciate the value of community in hearing God speak to us. We're part of the Body, and only when we live in submission to the other parts will we get the whole message. We can't demand our independence and expect to hear clearly the word for the Body.

"And of course, another factor is our trivializing the Scripture. We've dishonored it by reading our own ideas into it and then using its authority to back up our preconceived doctrines."

"Can we take the commands of Scripture personally?" Chuck wanted to know. "I mean, can I just find one of the commands of Jesus and obey it, expecting the miraculous power of the Word to work?"

"There are some conditions to consider," Uncle Herm responded. "First, does the command include you as its object? For instance, Jesus told His disciples in Luke 10:4 that they shouldn't take a change of clothes or moneybag with them on their missionary journey while He was still on earth. There was a specific purpose for their mission and that purpose was fulfilled. The gospel was first offered to the Jews—this journey was to fulfill that purpose. Later, the gospel was given to gentiles. Now this is no longer a command for anyone going out for missionary purposes.

"Again, Jesus told His disciples in Acts 1:4-5 to wait in Jerusalem for the enduement with the power of the Holy Spirit. Pentecost came on schedule and we no longer wait for that event.

"But Jesus said that we are part of His Body, so we can receive any commands given to the Body. He commanded us all to love and believe and forgive. Through the New Testament writers He has instructed us in how to pray, to heal the sick, proclaim the gospel, live in community, and solve problems. When the commands of Scripture fit us, we have the opportunity to act on them and expect God to fulfill His Word.

"Secondly, are you viewing the command as a requirement for acceptance, a detached mandate, a standard to measure up to, or is it a word from the heart of your Lord?

133

It's Jesus the living Word who does the work. We can no more live up to detached commands of Jesus than the Israelites could live up to the commands given through Moses. A written command is an opportunity to commune with the living Spirit who can make it a personal word to your heart."

"That does help," Francis added. "Can I ask for a command?"

"Sure." Uncle Herm nodded. "In Matthew 14:28-30, when Peter was in the boat with the other disciples during a storm, he saw Jesus walking on the water. Desiring to live as Jesus in that situation, he asked for a command. 'Command me to walk,' he requested. Jesus responded to his request with a word that endued Peter with the power to walk on the water. I think we should ask for commands if we're willing to obey them when they come. He probably won't give a command for us to vote on. Actually, we should ask for commands relating to those areas where we need divine intervention.

"I spoke to one man who had battled addictions for years. He tried every form of accountability treatment. Though he had been greatly helped by those, he longed to be free inside. He asked God diligently for a command. As he believed, God spoke to his heart, 'Be free!' He was able to do what he had never been able to do before.

"I realize someone can use this illustration to conclude we should all run down to the clinic and tell everyone, 'Be free!' and expect them all to get well. But remember, Jesus went to one man at the pool. He spoke a personal word to him. The faith that came from that personal word is what energized the man's obedience. God's word to someone else should encourage us to approach Him for our own word. He does want our personal faith in Him, not just detached words."

"So can we say that this is 'living in the Spirit'?" Chuck wondered.

"Yes, I think so," nodded Uncle Herm. "The Spirit lives inside us to make our inheritance real. He is the one who leads us into truth and empowers us to do the works of God. The commands of Jesus become personal through the work of the Holy Spirit."

"I really like this," Paul sighed contentedly. "I'm beginning to see how we can actually live like Jesus did. He had access to the Father through the Spirit, and now we have the same access. I need to get where I hear more clearly. I think I need to start believing that God actually speaks to me like He did to Jesus."

Uncle Herm smiled.

Uncle Herm's Homework

1. How many ways do we hear the voice of our Shepherd? Read John 10:1-5.

2. What reasons do we commonly give for the absence of miraculous power today?

3. How does submission in the Body of Christ relate to hearing God's Word?

4. What do you think the "sign" of the loaves was all about? Read John chapter 6.

5. How do purpose and passion relate in your life?

6. What do you feel "called" to do?

CHAPTER 13

Serious About Change

Kristy's face revealed some deep emotions going on inside. She had a different look in her dark brown eyes, a look of fearful discovery.

"What's up with you?" Paul asked with concern. "Are you okay?"

"I'm fine, I think. But to tell you the truth, I think for the first time this stuff is really getting to me. I mean, it's going beyond the discussion stage for me. If I really believe what I've been hearing, it will require some radical change in my approach to life."

"What exactly are you referring to?" Chuck asked as he looked around the room, hoping that he was not the only one who didn't quite understand what Kristy was talking about. "All of us are being challenged to rethink why we're here and what it all means."

"Yeah, but it just hit me this week that I've bought into the super-tolerant mentality that's permeating our culture. You know...the 'nobody is right and nobody is wrong' stuff that we all hear. I've been watching with great interest the controversy among some of the major Christian denominations. They're fighting over what one side calls tolerance and the other calls absolutes. After our last discussion, I've started thinking that the real issue is whether or not we Christians really believe people can change. I don't mean just get better, but change. Can homosexuals really change their orientation? Can addicts ever really have victory over their addictions? I guess I've been forced to even wonder if selfish people can ever be unselfish— can *I* change?"

"Listen to this," Uncle Herm said as he opened the New Testament and read slowly.

> *May grace and peace be multiplied to you in the knowledge of God and of Jesus our Lord. His divine power has granted to us all things that pertain to life and godliness, through the knowledge of Him who called us to His own glory and excellence, by which He has granted to us His precious and very great promises, so that through them you may become par-takers of the divine nature, having escaped from the corruption that is in the world because of sinful desire* (2 Peter 1:2-4).

"Sounds like we have some hope here to me."

"Yeah, that sounds good," agreed Chuck, "but really not many people change and stay changed. I know some who tes-tify of change but even they have issues that they don't seem to ever get settled."

Uncle Herm smiled to himself. He was glad things were now beginning to get down to where they lived. Discussion was turning into decision. "Remember, we talked about the radical gospel that produced a radical people who did radi-cal things. We agreed that something was wrong with the way we moderns and post-moderns approach the gospel. Religion is worthy of discussion and debate, but we have conveniently categorized it into pretty much a harmless compartment of life."

Kristy was still in a very serious mood. "I agree with what you're saying, but just exactly how does that fit with what we're talking about now?"

Uncle Herm continued. "Well, when we allow some other cause to possess us other than the glory of Christ; and when we accept some solution to mankind's problem that ignores the cross; and when we place some community above the Church, which is the living Body of Christ, we come up with a religion that is powerless, purposeless, and easily dismissed.

"In my experience, I've discovered several approaches to change. First, you can stay the same and hide. This is probably the most common. Shame is a powerful force, and many of us have tried to hide our weaknesses and perversions for fear that exposure would be too much to bear. Usually there comes a time when the pressure of the hiding becomes too much and some disclosure is made. This relieves the guilt of hypocrisy and opens the door for real change, but this alone doesn't go far enough to cut the root of the problem. Accountability to those who will not let us live in the darkness is healthy, but there has to be more."

Paul's head jerked up. "Is that what happens to so many people who are in programs for breaking addictions? I mean, they seem to have such a breakthrough when they come clean, but lots go back and are more hopeless than ever."

"I sure wouldn't want to speak against any programs that are helping people face their problems," Francis said as she sat up on the edge of her rocking chair.

"Of course not," Uncle Herm confirmed as he continued. "There's no way to count the numbers of people who have been helped through 12-step type programs. Those who have embraced these are to be commended with the highest of admiration. But every one of them would grieve with you over

139

the ones who don't change. They would also testify that sin management is not what they're all about. They know that one who only comes out of hypocrisy but not out of bondage has not embraced the whole concept."

"What are the other alternatives you were going to tell us?" Chuck was anxious to hear the rest.

"The second approach is to change the definition of what is normal. It's an attitude that says if we can't fix it, then it must be normal. Homosexuality was declared a normal alternative some years back by some psychological experts convinced they couldn't 'fix' it. What if we did the same to cancer? If cancer was reclassified as normal simply because it couldn't be cured, thousands would die because research would stop. I'm afraid that many Christians have reclassified their inheritance from God. They've concluded that misery and boredom are normal and that even Jesus doesn't fix that. So they put off to the next life what could be enjoyed now."

Kristy's brown eyes widened. "That really is the issue with the denominational squabbles, isn't it? I mean, if we really can't offer the hope of change to people who have serious issues, then we are a bit cruel to reject them for it. If it is behavior they can't change, we are being judgmental to classify them as unacceptable."

"I think you're right, Kristy." Uncle Herm was delighted to see the connections being made. "Unless we practice a gospel that really changes people, we're cruel to condemn them for unacceptable vices when we have acceptable ones."

Chuck was impatient. "Is there another approach to change?"

"Yes, you can change! That's the big step. If we don't believe we can change, we'll never take the steps necessary to accomplish it. The big question is: How?"

Paul was slyly snickering. "Maybe just getting old will help. I mean, there are some things we learn with time, and let's face it, some desires diminish with age." He gestured broadly at the look on Kristy's face. "I'm only half serious. I believe there's more to it than that, but it does seem to take time for us to either figure it out or to come to grips with our own issues."

Francis was quick to reply. "I don't want to wait that long. I'd like to have such an encounter with God that I got fixed— you know like the apostle Paul on the road to Damascus..."

"Or do we wait for another coming of Jesus to take us to that level?" Chuck interjected. "Is what we want only available in Heaven?"

"There are few 'quick fixes' in life." Uncle Herm was trying hard to suppress his delight in their vigorous interest in change. "But you can rest assured that God wants us to change. He is on schedule in making us in His image—while on earth. The ultimate Man, Jesus, showed us that life is to be lived in utter dependence on God the Father. He said that He didn't do or say anything that didn't come from the Father. In the Old Testament, particularly Deuteronomy 8:1-6, the explanation for leading Israel through the wilderness of temptation was to teach them to live by the word of God."

"So faith is the issue?" asked Kristy. "But then it seems that getting enough faith is as heavy a burden as the problem that needs faith to solve it."

"That can be the dilemma. Maybe we could find a definition of faith that doesn't lend itself to becoming another standard to be reached. Let me suggest one: Acting on God's word in God's time for God's glory. That can be just a cute cliché, but those are the elements in real faith.

"I think the best metaphor for faith is laughter. Real laughter is a response. If you initiate it, it's false. You can't laugh until something is funny. So you can't believe until there is something to believe. If faith is a spiritual reality, then our spirit must be touched before we can believe. Romans 10:17 says, 'Faith comes by hearing the word of Christ.' Then we must realize that we're not running the agenda and telling God what to do. We operate on His time schedule. For instance, Jesus came into the world as the Messiah on time. It was not the faith of the Jews that caused Him to come at that particular time.

"The last element of faith is the goal. Making Jesus famous is the issue for the Father and for us. It was the issue for Jesus while on earth, and He said it was why He could hear the voice of the Father so clearly. Read John 12:44-50. Biblical faith is not Heaven's credit card for us to spend on our own agendas. Our greatest fulfillment will come as we live for the glory of God."

Paul's brow furrowed. "There's a Scripture that seems strange to me. It's where Jesus and the disciples were talking about the hypocrite fig tree. Do you know which one? You know, Jesus had cursed it the day before and when they came back by, it was dried up from the roots. Jesus told them that if they had faith, they could speak to a mountain and it would move into the sea. Then He concluded with the perplexing statement, 'Therefore I tell you, whatever you ask in prayer, believe that you have received it and it will be yours.' It seems that the words should be reversed. If you have already received it, then you don't need to believe, do you?"

"That's a great point," Uncle Herm beamed. "It's the same point in the verses I read a few minutes ago. We've been given a package of resources. Now we can unpack it with faith. Since we have a vital relationship with the 'I AM' God, we already have what we need. Now we can access it by believing that we already have it. All we have to do is to determine the timing and that comes through real communion.

"Have you noticed in the Old Testament that the focus of worship is the altar? One can go no farther in the tabernacle of meeting or the temple until he goes to the altar. In the New Testament the focus seems to shift to the table. The altar has been filled with the final sacrifice. Now the table is prepared for God's people. The greatest honor we can show Him is to come to the table and eat. To delay is dishonor. To beg off because we feel disqualified is dishonor. The only right thing to do is come and eat. God is glorified when we receive what He has provided."

"But just how do we receive by faith? I guess I just get lost in the language somehow." The whole group nodded as Paul voiced their question.

"Let's use Mary, the mother of Jesus, as an illustration. The angel gave her God's word and indicated the time was at hand. So she had the basis for faith. Somehow she recognized that God would perform His word in her as she received it as done. Though she did not receive the seed of a man in conception, she received the seed of God's word and became pregnant. The moment she said 'yes' to God's word, she was pregnant. The birth did not come until nine months later, but the deed was done. Maybe our change happens like that. We receive the word of God and conceive. It may require some time before 'the baby is born.'

"Also, remember, faith is always a fight! Because the word of God is above the observation of natural senses, it appears to be contradictory. What we see and hear with our senses will fight the word of God. Others who are mainly ruled by the senses will join against the choice to believe. The fight is good because it will purify our faith and will strengthen our resolve to walk to please only Him."

Francis joined the discussion. "So how can we know the timing? That seems to be the most difficult part of the equation to me. I mean, I can know God's Word and desire to live for His glory, but how do I know I'm operating on His timetable?"

Uncle Herm got up slowly and stroked his chin. He was only stretching his back, but it added to the anticipation of his answer. "Well, any command that applies to us for daily living is a seed ready to be received. Any promise that includes us is a seed to be received."

"Like what exactly?" Chuck joined Uncle Herm standing.

"Love your enemies. The time is now. Forgive! We don't have to wait for another time to be obedient, and obedience is a miracle work of faith."

"What about the promises?" Paul asked. "How do you know which ones you can appropriate? I've seen people just going through Scripture picking out promises. They seem to always avoid those that promise judgment or wrath on misbehavior."

"A good point," Uncle Herm said as he settled into the rocker again. "The big promise that dominates history is fulfilled in the coming of Jesus. He is the ultimate Savior-King. He creates the new people who get the full inheritance. When He ascended and then sent the Holy Spirit to indwell believers, He was fulfilling the promise that had long captured the hope of Israel.

"Listen to Peter in his sermon at Pentecost. 'Being therefore exalted at the right hand of God, and having received from the Father the promise of the Holy Spirit, He has poured out this that you yourselves are seeing and hearing....Repent and be baptized every one of you in the name of Jesus Christ for the forgiveness of your sins, and you will receive the gift of the

Holy Spirit. For the promise is for you and for your children and for all who are far off, everyone whom the Lord our God calls to Himself' (Acts 2:33,38-39).

"The indwelling Holy Spirit makes all the promises available to us. He delivers the fellowship with God necessary to hear His voice. He empowers us to do what we alone could not do. Remember, it was by the power of the Spirit that Jesus was raised from the dead. That same power is available to change us and empower us to live differently. Can I say it again? We can spend our lives unpacking the treasure we have in Christ. He has moved inside. We don't need to go to the temple. We—plural—are the temple.

"Do you remember the FedEx commercial on TV during Super Bowl XXXVII? It was a take-off of the movie *Castaway*. In the movie, Tom Hanks plays a FedEx pilot whose plane crashes, which strands him on a deserted island for years. In the commercial, a FedEx employee looking like the scruffy rescued survivor approaches the door of a suburban home with a package in his hand. When the door is opened, he hands the package to the lady and explains that he has been stuck on an island for five years, but kept the package safe to deliver it to her. She replies with a simple 'Thank you.'

"He's curious as to what is in this package that he protected so vigorously and asks the lady what's inside.

"She opens it and shows him the contents saying, 'Oh nothing really. Just a satellite telephone, a global positioning device, a compass, a water purifier, and some seeds.'

"Are we holding a package that contains all we need to accomplish all that we desire? Have we been waiting for a day that has already come? Are we looking for an experience to do for us what we won't let God do by the power of His word?"

145

Kristy had been soaking all this in and wanted to believe. "So can you sum this up? Can you maybe suggest how we can start the process of transformation?"

"I think you've brought up some good points and suggestions. The key point is to stop fantasizing and believe that what we need has already been given. Oh, I would caution that you might first consider what you want to change into. If God changes us, it will be a change into people who live for someone other than ourselves. If you don't want a lifestyle of giving and serving, you should not ask God for change. I believe all of you want that, but some just want to get rid of the particular perversions that hinder their narcissistic lifestyles. They want to be free of bondage, but not free from selfishness.

"Then it's important to practice what you believe about God living inside. If He does, then every effort should be made to fellowship with Him. It's the consciousness of His presence that gives us faith to go on.

"When I was taking flying lessons, I had a wonderful instructor who was a retired colonel in the Air Force. He was very demanding, and I wasn't sure if I would ever qualify to solo. One day I ventured out. 'When do you think I'll be ready to solo?' 'Oh, maybe next Friday,' he said. So the next Monday we were doing some touch-and-go's when he asked me to stop the plane. He got out and said, 'Take her around. You're ready.' I almost swallowed my heart. Both fear and excitement filled me. I remember looking over at the empty seat he had just vacated. 'Jesus,' I said, 'it's just You and me. I know You know how to fly, and I need all Your attention right now.' It was a thrilling few moments of worship as I flew the plane and successfully landed it.

"I seek to live each day with that kind of desperation and joyful expectation. I know it's not about learning new secrets and following new formulas. It's all about living with Jesus as the real resurrected Lord.

"And then I would recommend that we trust more than we try. I mean, after a full commitment to change, we must stop trying to change while we trust the One who changes us. Then we should act like changed people. The pregnancy comes before the birth."

Uncle Herm's Homework

1. Read carefully Romans 6:6-14. What does it mean to "reckon" or "consider" yourself dead to sin and alive to Christ?

2. How did you become addicted to sin? (answer in the passage)

3. How can you change your addiction? (answer in the passage)

4. Read Second Peter 1:1-14. In the list of what is included in the package, which one do you need most right now? It is probably time to trust.

5. In the discussion of this chapter, what thought captured your attention?

6. What is the difference in trying and trusting?

CHAPTER 14

The Present Future

By their next meeting, there was definitely a hint of spring in the air. Although there was a nip in the breeze, the group couldn't resist sitting on the porch in the sunlight. Everyone was quiet today, listening to the sounds of the new season.

Francis took a deep breath. "You don't think that what's on this earth is all there is, do you? I mean—there is a Heaven, a future—isn't there?"

"The good news keeps getting better," Uncle Herm smiled. "We live in an age when the future has broken into the present. We get to enjoy the benefits of the future now without losing the future."

Kristy was perplexed. "What does that mean?"

"We live in the age to come while it is coming." Everyone looked at Uncle Herm, not sure how to respond. "Remember, Jesus referred to it in the parables of the Kingdom. It's like leaven that works surely, though slowly and unnoticed by the naked eye, toward filling the whole lump. It's like the small mustard seed that grows to a stature that the birds of the air can use. It starts off small and insignificant but progresses to something that benefits all the nations. We are in that process that Jesus talks about in Matthew 13:31-33."

"That sounds like good news for now, but what about our future?" Paul wanted to know.

Uncle Herm leaned forward in his rocker and spoke earnestly. "We have the privilege of doing our part and then passing the baton to following generations who can build on what we've done. When our time on earth is over, we are given bodies that will correspond to our new environment in Heaven. You can read about it in First Corinthians 15:35-54."

"What will that be like?" Paul asked.

"Unfortunately for our inquisitive minds, there isn't a chapter in the Bible that specifically tells us all about Heaven." Uncle Herm settled back into his chair. "Some would take parts of the Revelation of John and interpret it as a literal description of Heaven. I think Heaven is so grand that mere words can't describe it. We have to talk about it in symbols that reflect beauty, majesty, splendor, and glory. It's enough that we will be in the unclouded presence of God. No wonder we will need new bodies." Uncle Herm laughed apologetically and patted himself on the chest. "These are not equipped for that kind of glory. But, you know what? I think when we get to Heaven, it will be familiar."

"Now there's a mind-bender," Paul interjected.

"Well, we've lived in the Kingdom of God on earth and we've experienced the eternal life provided by Jesus," Uncle Herm said by way of explanation. "The limitations will be gone, but the essence of life will be the same. That's why we should be diligent in getting accustomed to the culture of the Kingdom now instead of living simply by the rules of mammon. Maybe to some it will be a strange land, but for those saints who have appropriated the superior lifestyle offered in Christ, it won't be totally strange."

"You hear all the songs about Heaven and the reunion of loved ones. Will it really be like that?" Kristy wanted to know.

Uncle Herm shrugged slightly. "I really don't know how all that will work. I think anything eternal we've experienced here will still be in existence there, but with more intensity. For instance, love does not die. Those we have loved here will be loved there, just without the mixture. Faith does not die, nor does hope. So all those will characterize life then. It will be better than we can imagine. Paul said in Philippians 1:21-26 that it would be his choice to go on but it was necessary for him to stay on earth to fulfill his assignment."

"Why shouldn't we all want to go to Heaven right now?" Kristy asked honestly.

"Paul's words should help us with that question," Uncle Herm began. "His point is that living with Jesus for the glory of God is the issue. It doesn't matter if it's in this body or in the next one. 'To live is Christ; to die is gain.' If we've set our goal to glorify Him, we're focused on doing our assignment knowing that even death can't defeat us.

"There is something inside us all that longs for the unclouded day. We're made for unobstructed fellowship with God. While on the earth with the corruption from the fall of mankind, we 'look through a clouded glass,' according to First Corinthians 13:12. Then we shall see clearly and know as we are known.

"There's also something inside that wants to express the life of Christ that's in us. We should spend our energies discovering how to give. Giving is the key to grace and grace is the heart of God. The more we learn how to give ourselves away, the more our souls will be fulfilled. We are designed for giving and we must live by design if we're to be truly free."

"Based on what I hear, for some people, Heaven would be an escape—not just the final reward," Kristy offered.

"It's true that some people see Heaven that way," Uncle Herm responded. "But Heaven is not designed to be our escape route. Heaven will be better then, after we have lived here in a heavenly way. Remember that death is not your deliverer; it is a conquered foe. Jesus is the deliverer, and He might want you to stay around for a while and enjoy the work of managing the earth."

"So our future is victory now and glory later!" Paul exclaimed.

"That's one way to put it," Uncle Herm smiled. "Remember that God's story never ends. The nature of His life is eternal. We are part of the eternal story of God. Some are worried or at least focused on the end of the world. A better focus is the purpose of God and how the world fits into it."

"So when does the world end?" Chuck wanted to know.

"We aren't told," Uncle Herm admitted. "Our life never ends. God never ends. What He does with the world will fit into His ultimate purposes."

"Should we be looking for the end of the world?" Paul asked.

"I don't." Uncle Herm's answer was firm. "I'm pretty sure my end of earthly existence will come before the world ends. It doesn't take the end of the world to sum everything up. God summed up everything in Jesus. The story is about Him, not the end of the world. There are lots of people living on this earth, and I'd like for them to have a chance to know God before the world ends. I'd also like for the Church to have a chance to express the Kingdom of God here before time is up.

"I really don't have time to worry about the end of the world. There's a God to know better, a world to subdue, a Church to grow up, and a time for me to die."

"What about Christ's second coming?" Paul asked. "Or, how did you put it—His last coming? How does that fit into our hope for the future? What do you think about First Thessalonians 4:13-18?"

"Paul the apostle addresses the issue of saints who had died previously," explained Uncle Herm. "Because the believers at Thessalonica are concerned about them, Paul assures the living saints that those who have died will not be left behind. When the Lord appears, they will be raised first and then those who are alive will join them."

Chuck jumped in. "I was taught that was the rapture."

"Whatever it's called, there's no mention of a secret rapture followed by seven years of tribulation and then another coming of Christ," noted Uncle Herm. "That would have to be imposed on the passage. The focus is on the sure hope of both the living and the dead saints. Jesus' resurrection assures both that His victory will be enjoyed forever, and they will always be with the Lord."

"But what about the part about the day of the Lord coming like a thief in the night?" Chuck persisted.

Uncle Herm continued. "Paul goes on to say in First Thessalonians 5:1-11 that his readers already know the expected judgment will come like a thief. He is clear, however, that they will not be victims of the thief. Only those who are asleep or drunk will be surprised by the sudden events. The 'children of light' will not be taken unaware. They are not destined to wrath but to salvation."

"Is he talking about 70 A.D. or the final day of the Lord?" Paul asked.

"Probably the events of 70 A.D. He has already mentioned in First Thessalonians 2:15-16 the wrath coming on the unbelieving Jews. The 'day of the Lord' is a phrase that depicts a coming judgment. Joel had used it in Joel 1:15 and 2:1 to describe the locust attack on Israel in his day, but also prophesied a future day. In Acts 2:16-21, Peter at Pentecost said Joel's prophecy was being fulfilled. Within a generation of Peter's sermon, God judged the real enemies of Christ using the Roman army just like He used the locust in Joel's day."

Paul was trying to sort things out. "So, the day of the Lord is judgment?"

"It's justice being finally meted out," Uncle Herm clarified. "God has great patience and will wait long periods, but finally He judges unrighteousness openly. The pattern is:

1. God's way proclaimed;

2. the people's disregard;

3. warning;

4. God's patience;

5. God uses an alien army, like locust or soldiers, to judge the people;

6. God judges the army;

7. God saves His repentant people. So, it's a day of both judgment and salvation.

"The Jews had looked forward to the day of the Lord because they had identified God's enemy as Rome. When the day came, the enemy was revealed as unbelieving Israel. Salvation came to the despised sect known as Jesus' followers. Finally, Christians were no longer identified with Judaism, and the rabid Jewish leaders were no longer around to persecute them. That day came on the Jews like a thief. They were totally unaware of what was happening."

"Is there another 'day of the Lord' coming?" Francis asked anxiously.

Uncle Herm nodded. "I think so. Since God has used the earth as the stage for His glory, I expect Him to conclude things on earth just as He began. The final day of the Lord will reveal Jesus in His unclouded fullness. Romans 8:17-18 says that those who have rejected Him will be exposed while those who follow Him will be exalted. And in Romans 2:16, you can read that eternal justice will be done on earth as in Heaven."

Uncle Herm's Homework

1. What's in our future? (Read 1 Corinthians 15.) List the benefits we are promised.

2. What "end" was Peter talking about? (Read 1 Peter 4:7.)

3. What "last hour" was in John's mind? (Read 1 John 2:18.)

4. What "day of the Lord" is Peter referring to? (Read 2 Peter 3:1-18.)

5. What was the issue in the judgment Jesus describes in Matthew 25:31-46?

CHAPTER 15

As Valuable as Noah

"Getting the bigger picture has sure been helpful," Paul began as the group once again gathered on Uncle Herm's front porch. "We've been told that the only story that really matters is our own story. You know, how we're living in a post-modern culture."

"Can somebody give me a good definition of *post-modern*?" Chuck asked. "I'm tired of being told that I'm post-modern and not knowing exactly what that means."

"It just means that we are not modern, right?" offered Francis. "I mean, we're past the modern era, and we reject the boundaries of modern thinking."

"Okay. Then define *modern*," Chuck persisted.

"I think Modernism has been defined in terms of reason, logic, and science," Francis explained hesitantly. "A common phrase for modernism is 'Scientists tell us....' For the most part, reality is bordered by man's reason, intellect, and personal experience. Is that right?"

"Pretty much, if I understand it," Paul offered. "*Post-modern* is a little harder to pin down, though. Remember, it's Post-modernism, with the emphasis on what it's not. Basically, it's a reaction to Modernism. I heard someone quoting Jean Francois Lyotard's definition as 'the incredulity of the meta-narrative.' As I understand that, it means there is skepticism toward any one story explaining the meaning of life, history, morals, etc."

"So everyone can have their own, individual explanations?" Kristy asked.

"Yes, exactly," Paul nodded. He was in his element. "For the post-modern, it would be highly presumptuous for anyone to assume knowledge of an over-arching story. Everyone's history is distinct and not necessarily linked to others."

Kristy shook her head. "No wonder we live with so much hopelessness. I mean, that might sound good on the surface, but it leaves the individual with all the responsibility to interpret everything and to find any purpose life might have. That's too much."

"I think breaking out of the tight box of Modernism is good, though," Francis argued. "Life is more than reason, logic, and the test tube. But Post-modernism seems to leave us adrift in a sea of questions without needed answers. Uncle Herm, what do you think?"

"We have a great story," he said simply.

"You mean the Bible?" Francis asked.

"Yes, the gospel that's contained in the Bible," Uncle Herm responded. "This story, or meta-narrative, if you will, is not some product of an overactive imagination. It's a recorded history. It explains the 'needed answers' you mentioned, Francis. There's an old gospel hymn written by Katherine Hankey that comes to mind." Uncle Herm leaned back and began to sing softly: " 'I love to tell the story of unseen things above; of Jesus and His glory; of Jesus and His love. I love to tell the story, because I know 'tis true. It satisfies my longings as nothing else can do.'"

There was a long pause before Paul asked quietly, "What if post-moderns refuse to accept the fact that there is a story?"

"That's *their* story," Uncle Herm said firmly. "We listen to them in order to earn the right to tell ours. Our story is true. It will find a home in the lonely, confused heart of the true seeker. Our real effectiveness will be living a life full of passion and purpose."

"So that means we need to really know the story," Paul stated.

"It means we must actually *live* the story," Uncle Herm corrected gently. "You've all heard about the 'book'—the one that contains the names of those who get into Heaven, right? You know the old picture of coming up to the pearly gates and being greeted by Saint Peter. He asks your name and then looks for it in the giant ledger. You wait anxiously for him to find it there, hoping that he will.

"What if the book is a narrative? Peter begins his search with Adam's time, then moves to Noah, Abraham, Moses, David, Ezra, Malachi, John the Baptist, Jesus, Stephen, Paul on through the years to the 21st century. 'Oh, there you are,' he says as he sees the part you played in the redemption story. 'You had a part to play just like Noah.'"

"Now that's a big idea." Paul was practically speechless.

"When God saved Noah, He did so to involve Noah in the ongoing story," Uncle Herm continued. "He didn't just save him to ignore him. Noah was a vital link in the 'meta-narrative.' He was used to show that destroying the world does not fix the heart of man. He started a whole new creation, thereby telling all generations that God is into new beginnings. He prefigured the coming 'Noah' and 'Last Adam' who would bring in another new creation made up

159

of all people whose hearts were washed clean by the blood of the final Lamb—not by the flood waters of destruction."

Francis was blown away. "I can't believe I'm as vital to God's purpose as Noah. That's too much of a stretch for me."

"Remember Hebrews chapter 11?" Uncle Herm prompted. "All the saints form a cloud of witnesses who watch us as we play out the narrative."

Francis shook her head in amazement. "That sure adds another dimension to finding my place."

Paul had a sudden thought. "Hey, that helps me understand the apostle Paul's attitude about life and death. He knew he had a part to play, and had some idea of what it looked like. He could live with abandon because he was indispensable until his work was done."

"But not everyone is as pivotal as Paul," Francis protested. "Some have lesser parts."

"True, but each part is important in focusing attention on the story's Star," said Uncle Herm.

"So, is that how we find our part in the story?" Paul wanted to know. "Just try to glorify Jesus?"

"I think it's important to know where in the story we live," Uncle Herm responded. "We're not Old Testament saints waiting for the big event. We live in the era of fulfillment, so our part involves embracing the new creation. The old era of promise has been fulfilled by the resurrection and the ascension of the Lord. We are the final temples of God on earth, and we have the privilege of being witnesses to the gospel that is powerful enough to transform people and culture."

Uncle Herm leaned forward, his voice filled with passion. "We are not waiting for a better day on earth to do the works of God. This is our day! We must stop looking for imminent destruction. God will finish His purpose on earth. So we're free to get involved in life and expect God to work through us to bring about His purpose. Each act of faith on our part can be as vital as Noah building the ark.

"You know, at first glance, building the ark was not a ministerial activity. Building an ark was a down and dirty act of manual labor. But, when done by faith, it saved the future. What if every believer did each act of work with the expectation that God would use it to further the plan? Don't you think that would add a sense of purpose and release more passion?"

"I think I see it," Chuck was getting excited. "That's what you mean about destroying the wall between the secular and the spiritual. Every act of life should be an act of faith. Wow! So I can focus on my talents and gifts and use them with the confidence that God will sovereignly guide me to the right place and let me honor Jesus with my own stuff."

"That's exactly right," Uncle Herm agreed, his eyes shining. "The story that began with God creating a world to glorify His Son will always be about a world that glorifies His Son. Our story tells of a creation, a fall in Adam and Eve, a covenant with the earth in Noah, a covenant with Abraham that would guarantee blessings to all peoples, a covenant with Moses that defined the people who would produce the servant Seed, a covenant with David that guarantees an eternal Kingdom of God that protects His people, and finally the Seed that becomes the new covenant, producing a people reborn by the Spirit of God."

Uncle Herm paused and looked at the group. "We are part of that people! And we still have work to do until the knowledge of the glory of God covers the world as the water covers the sea."

Uncle Herm's Homework

1. Read Hebrews 11 and tell how each witness mentioned there played a vital role in the story.

2. What is your role?

Epilogue

Once again, the Armageddon Discussion group gathered for a funeral. Almost 20 years had passed since the death of a friend had prompted their most serious soul-searching. Now, though a hint of sadness mingled through the crowd, there was also a sense of celebration. The Armageddon kids had returned to say good-bye to Uncle Herm for the last time. At the age of 94, their mentor and spiritual father had gone home.

Paul arrived from the Northeast, leaving his wife, Amy, to care for their three boys. Paul was now a professor of philosophy at an Ivy League school, committed to sharing the Kingdom principles with his own searching students.

From the opposite end of the country, Kristy flew in from Los Angeles where she was a television entertainment producer for a major studio. She and her husband, Steve, had put off starting a family for a while, but were now the proud parents of twin girls.

Chuck and Francis never left their hometown, deciding instead that God meant for them to be together there. Married for almost 15 years, they had two children who were just entering the exciting and challenging teenage years. Chuck owned a large business in town, overseeing hundreds of employees.

Francis was a stay-at-home mom—except when the state legislature was in session. Then three days a week she was

Madame Senator, working hard to pass laws that were compatible with Kingdom principles.

But now the four gathered in the visitation room of the funeral home, catching up and comparing family pictures before time for the funeral to begin.

"Somehow, it's not hard to picture you as a prof," Chuck teased Paul. "I *am* surprised you wound up at an Ivy League school, though. Do you ever feel out of place?"

"Oh, sure," Paul agreed. "I have friends there, but many times I feel ostracized because my views are out of the norm. But it's comforting to remember that my philosophies are actually much closer to those of the founding fathers at my university than those of my colleagues."

Francis and Kristy both nodded. "I certainly know what it feels like to be outside the norm," Kristy smiled. "Try being a card-carrying, Kingdom believer in Tinseltown. It's a different world. But I love what I do, and I know I'm where I'm supposed to be. Someone's got to stand up for decent entertainment that means something but doesn't preach."

"And as someone who works with college students, I can't tell you how important it is to have you putting out shows that don't cater to the lowest common denominator," Paul remarked. "What you're doing really matters."

"Francis, you're in the same boat we are, aren't you?" Kristy asked.

"Different venue, same basic story," Francis nodded. "Too many people with egos, not enough statesmen." She smiled at herself. "Or stateswomen. But we need to be in the mix. The laws we pass are for everyone, and it's exciting to see Kingdom principles at work in the political arena. They really work!"

Epilogue

"Must be tough on you when they're in session, though," Paul interjected sympathetically to Chuck.

"Well, we have our moments!" Chuck agreed with a laugh. "And it can be a real balancing act at times. But I know that God's calling on Francis to be in that arena, and it's worth all the sacrifice to see what a difference she makes."

"Of course, Chuck won't tell you much about his business," Francis jumped in, "but it's amazing what he's accomplished. He has really turned the company around, and made it profitable while gaining the reputation of being honest and forthright. And his employees love him—he works so hard to be fair and equitable with them. He really cares about them and they know it."

Kristy shook her head. "It's pretty amazing, isn't it? Those talks with Uncle Herm really did make a difference." She looked around at the small group. "I mean, look at us. We're all in different places in society, different career paths, different struggles, but all affecting those around us for the Kingdom."

"Do you ever feel like sometimes people in the church are the ones who don't understand?" Francis asked Kristy.

"Oh, yes," Kristy said emphatically. "The television industry just doesn't look like the 'narrow way' they're used to. Or they think that the only 'good' programming is Christian programming, and Christian programming is only 'good' if it preaches. They can't see that sometimes the most important thing is to just get people thinking."

"I'm asked by well-meaning believers all the time why I'm not teaching at a Christian school or at a seminary," Paul remarked. "I remind them that Jesus Himself said He came for the sick, not the well. But truthfully, there are also students who come to college believing, then get beaten into the dust by humanistic professors. I try to help them keep their eyes on the real goal. I know that's part of why I'm there. Higher education is a very dark place—even a small light can make a difference."

"It's the same with me," Francis added. "Church members sometimes remind me that a woman's place is in the home, not the political arena. But I know it's my place because it's where God called me, and that gives me the courage to stand there—thanks to Uncle Herm and his teaching. Uncle Herm's teachings helped me avoid falling into the trap of shallow, politically expedient, liberal-versus-conservative debates. Instead, he taught me to apply the Kingdom principle of finding long-term solutions to long-term problems."

Chuck nodded. "What I learned from Uncle Herm helped me see that being a good businessman is more than just holding a Bible study before work. And it's not just about making money—even making money for a special project or mission—even though that's not bad. Real Kingdom business is conducting business with a purpose."

"That's the key," Paul added. "That's the message Uncle Herm gave us. God gives purpose to our lives. Find your purpose, then do it with all your heart."

The four of them sat together throughout the funeral; then Chuck stood up to deliver the closing thoughts on behalf of their little group.

"Twenty years ago, when I first met Uncle Herm, as we called him, I was just a confused college kid," Chuck began. "I had a lot of ill-conceived theologies and bad doctrines. I didn't have a lot of hope, and even thought maybe it would be better not to try at all.

"But for some reason, Uncle Herm saw fit to invest in my life, and in the lives of some of my friends. He listened to us, taught us, and guided us until we were able to lead on our own. In us, he saw the future.

"He taught us that what we believe matters; that we have a destiny, a God-given calling on our lives; that hope is alive and well; that we *can* make a difference. And because he invested in us, even though his physical body is gone, his legacy lives on...in us. Every life we touch is because he touched us. And this will continue generationally for years, and decades, and even centuries. Uncle Herm has left me with the determination to be an 'Uncle Herm' to someone else..."

Chuck paused for a moment to regain his composure, then brought his thoughts to a close. "But the last thing Uncle Herm would want today is for us to focus on him. He spent his entire life focusing on the One who brings Life. From today, let's go out and make a difference. Let's take the Kingdom into the marketplace, into the schools, into government. We have to let people know that there is hope; that there is life; that there is purpose. God has left us behind for a reason—and I'm glad to be a part of what He's doing on earth today."

The organ music surged as the congregation filed out into the bright sunshine, and another generation took the Kingdom message on.

APPENDIX A

Honoring Israel and Exalting Jesus

Since the Garden of Eden, there has been a battle against the people of God. When the enemy hasn't been able to destroy them by annihilation, he has tried to confuse their identity. Today the battle still rages. There is much confusion as to the real identity of God's people. Some are convinced that God has two peoples: one an earthly natural people defined by race and geography, another defined by spirit and Heaven. One is natural Israel and the other is the Church. There are voices filling the air calling people back to facets of Judaism with the promise that God will bless that which relates to natural Israel. Some Christians are so taken with the purposes of political Israel, they seem to have lost the supremacy of Jesus who is the ultimate Israelite and the head of the Church which is His Body.

Some of the confusion comes from the failure to recognize the continuity of the Old Testament and the New Testament. If we do not interpret the Old in light of the New, we will inevitably conclude that God has unfinished business with natural Israel. If, however, we see that the New fulfills the Old, we will see the whole story as one of God's people being a people of faith from first to last. In Romans 9–11, the most specific passage regarding the identity of God's people and the purpose of natural Israel, the apostle seems to be showing the distinction between believing Israel and natural Israel.

> *But it is not as though the Word of God has failed. For not all who are descended from Israel belong to Israel, and not all are children of Abraham because they are his offspring, but "through Isaac shall your offspring be named." This means that it is not the children of the flesh who are the children of God, but the children of the promise are counted as offspring* (Romans 9:6-8).

God has always worked through the people who believed Him according to His revelation of Himself. There were numerous seeds of Abraham who were not part of the chosen people. Only the remnant who believed were recipients of God's favor.

And Isaiah cries out concerning Israel: "Though the number of the sons of Israel be as the sand of the sea, only a remnant of them will be saved" (Rom. 9:27).

The accusation that is usually leveled at someone who broaches this subject is, "That is replacement theology!" This is often said with the implication that such a view is tantamount to being anti-Semitic. Actually it is not replacement, but fulfillment. The "new man" made up of believing Jews and gentiles does not replace Israel. The Church *fulfills* the purposes of God that He initiated with a faith-covenant with Abraham.

> *For He Himself is our peace, who has made us both one and has broken down in His flesh the dividing wall of hostility by abolishing the law of commandments and ordinances, that He might create in Himself one new man in place of the two, so making peace, and might reconcile us both to God in one body through the cross, thereby killing the hostility. And He came and preached peace to you who were far off and peace to those who were near. For through Him we both have access in one Spirit to the Father* (Ephesians 2:14-18).

Israel served the world by demonstrating the inability of man to be righteous by keeping law, and by producing the Messiah who would bless the world by giving His life as a ransom. Now that Messiah has come, all people of the earth have access to God and His righteousness on the same ground—faith in Jesus the Messiah. The Church is God's focus, and it is through the Church that the principalities in the heavenlies marvel at God's wisdom.

> *So that through the church the manifold wisdom of God might now be made known to the rulers and authorities in the heavenly places. This was according to the eternal purpose that He has realized in Christ Jesus our Lord* (Ephesians 3:10-11).

Some make a big issue of the phrase: "All Israel will be saved" (Rom. 11:26) interpreting this reference as natural Israel. However, Paul has just defined Israel as those Jews and gentiles who come to faith in Jesus as Israel's Messiah and the world's Savior. His point is that all who come to God through Jesus the Messiah are defined as true Israel, and they all must come by faith. This is the way all Israel will be saved—by faith. This new nation of faith-people is God's Israel.

The New Testament is silent about the restoration of Israel as a political entity. Jesus came to reveal to His own that their hope was better than they expected. They had hoped for a restored nation, and He came to give them eternal life. Most could never see it. They believed He was a heretic because He did not submit to their literal interpretation of land and temple. They were so focused on real estate and the physical temple in Jerusalem, they could not see the bigger picture of God having a people defined by Spirit and love. Remember, God had first made the covenant with Abraham with the intention of blessing the whole world through the seed of Abraham. The Jews were insistent that the issue was still land and temple.

Paul was hounded because he preached that the hope of Israel was Jesus and the resurrection He provided for all believers. His Jewish enemies accused him of being against the temple, the law, and the Jews.

> *When the seven days were almost completed, the Jews from Asia, seeing him in the temple, stirred up the whole crowd and laid hands on him, crying out, "Men of Israel, help! This is the man who is teaching everyone everywhere against the people and the law and this place. Moreover, he even brought Greeks into the temple and has defiled this holy place"* (Acts 21:27-28).

They too could not see that God had fulfilled His promises in a fuller way than they had expected. The big event that created the "new man" was the Christ-event. When the Holy Spirit came, He made every believer a temple of God, and He fulfilled the demands of the law by imparting the power of love. Rather than establishing the nation of Israel as separate and superior to other nations, the big event of the New Testament destroyed the distinctions that divided Jew and gentile and made one new nation out of the two.

This is something that has already been done. It is not some future event that we hope for. We do not have to wait for another event in Palestine in order to see this dynamic in action. We activate it by faith now. Our hope now is that the gospel of Jesus will be proclaimed and believed among both Jew and gentile. Paul hoped that the superior life demonstrated by Christians would make Jews jealous. That is our hope and goal. Their inclusion will come the same as all the world—through faith in Jesus. The New Testament offers no hope for anyone finding righteousness apart from faith in Jesus as the already revealed Son of God, Messiah, and Savior.

Paul's warning was against arrogance.

But if some of the branches were broken off, and you, although a wild olive shoot, were grafted in among the others and now share in the nourishing root of the olive tree, do not be arrogant toward the branches. If you are, remember it is not you who support the root, but the root that supports you. Then you will say, "Branches were broken off so that I might be grafted in." That is true. They were broken off because of their unbelief, but you stand fast through faith. So do not become proud, but stand in awe. For if God did not spare the natural branches, neither will He spare you. Note then the kindness and the severity of God: severity toward those who have fallen, but God's kindness to you, provided you continue in His kindness. Otherwise you too will be cut off. And even they, if they do not continue in their unbelief, will be grafted in, for God has the power to graft them in again. For if you were cut from what is by nature a wild olive tree, and grafted, contrary to nature, into a cultivated olive tree, how much more will these, the natural branches, be grafted back into their own olive tree (Romans 11:17-24).

Gentiles were grafted into the branch of believing Israel because they believed. Israel was broken off because of unbelief. It can be reversed. There is no room for boasting for either. Jews do not need to become gentiles to be saved, and gentiles do not need to become Jews. All must come humbly to trust in Jesus who did for us what we could not do for ourselves. There is no hope for anyone who tries to come in another way or at another time.

Our attitude toward natural Israel should be one of gratitude. Jesus told the Samaritan woman, "...salvation is from the Jews. Yet a time is coming and has now come when the true worshipers will worship the Father in spirit and truth..." (Jn. 4:22-23). It was through Israel that the Messiah came and offered salvation to the whole world. Israel as God's servant has blessed the whole world as God promised Abraham initially.

Humility is also appropriate. If Israel was broken off because of unbelief, we too can be deceived by pride. No race or culture has a patent on God's favor. He has fulfilled His plan to conclude all people as sinners who are desperately needy so He could reveal to them the majestic mercy of Jesus the Son. God has not blessed or cursed on the basis of race, but faith— faith in God as revealed through Jesus the Son.

As believers we must also be compassionate and willing to share the only way of salvation with all people of all nations. Jews should not be required to become gentiles, but they can't substitute their traditions for faith in Jesus as Christ. They deserve the gospel. If we put them into a special category that bypasses Christ and the cross, we deny our own faith and dishonor them.

In today's confusion we must also be cautious. We cannot afford to mix political Zionism with biblical theology. (Zionism refers to the 19th-century movement to establish a homeland for displaced Jews in the land of Palestine. It was fueled by the belief that Israel had a divine right to the land. There is continued emphasis on political Israel's favored position with God.) The special treatment of political entities on the basis of anything but justice goes against God's Kingdom. God's favor is not meted out on the basis of our attitude toward political Israel, but our attitude toward His Son. Political values must be based on the same foundation as God's government: justice and truth. We belong to a Kingdom that supercedes all governments of the earth and are brothers with all who belong to this Kingdom ruled by Jesus the Lord. It is the household of faith that demands our loyalty. We stand together with men and women from all nations, tribes, and cultures who have faith in our God who has revealed Himself in Jesus.

We must also be cautious about elevating our historical roots over the absolutes of Christian dogma. It is interesting and valuable to discover the beautiful types and shadows of biblical Judaism. Too many gentiles have robbed themselves of the rich heritage of the Old Testament. All believers want to find meaning in the big story. We want to know how we today relate to Abraham, Moses, David, and Jeremiah. When the big story is not told, we tend to magnify Jewish customs, maybe in an effort to get in touch with our roots. But we tend to swing from one extreme to another. Jewish customs do not make us more or less righteous. When the focus turns from magnifying Jesus to fascination with Israel, Jewish customs, Torah, or speculations about future temples and wars, there is big danger. Legalism and literalism are always detrimental to true faith. Speculation about Old Testament prophecies being fulfilled in our day is dangerous. Jesus is the "yes and amen" of God's promises. If New Testament authors did not explain the Old Testament in light of Jesus, we are presumptuous to think we can explain it without their help.

Jesus gave us permission to judge by the fruit. If we find ourselves preoccupied with anything other than the Star of God's universe, we should examine our faith. Jesus is the agent and goal of all creation. True faith in God will always leave us kneeling at His cross and worshipping.

APPENDIX B

Signs of the End—Matthew 24

The passage that is most used to describe the signs of the end is Matthew 24, with parallel passages in Mark 13 and Luke 21. But the vital question is: End of what?

Jesus has just delivered His most scathing rebuke on the Jerusalem leaders who had revealed their hearts of rebellion by their rejection of Jesus. He pronounced a series of "woes" on them and declared, "Truly, I say to you, all these things will come upon this generation" (Mt. 23:36). He then speaks to all of Jerusalem and declares, "Your house will be left desolate." Then He leaves the temple, and His disciples are pointing out the beauty of the temple buildings. He declares emphatically: "There will not be left here one stone upon another that will not be thrown down" (Mt. 24:2).

This astounds the disciples who follow Him to the Mount of Olives and question Him regarding His statement. "Tell us, when will these things be, and what will be the sign of Your coming and of the close of the age?" (Mt. 24:3) It is this question that Jesus answers in the following verses. After describing some observable events that will occur—false Christs, struggles among nations, earthquakes, persecution of believers, the spread of the gospel to the known world, the abomination of desolation, tribulation, signs in heavens, and judgment—He again says that "this generation will not pass away until all these things take place" (Mt. 24:34).

Whole books have been written on this passage. Here I will make a few observations.

1. There is no clear evidence that Jesus is answering three different questions put to Him by His disciples. They are concerned about one thing—the destruction of the city and the temple.

2. The preaching of the gospel of the Kingdom to the whole known world was accomplished in that generation (see Col. 1:6; Rom. 10:18).

3. The abomination of desolation was something that happened while that generation was alive. They were told where to run for escape and to hope that it would not be on a sabbath. Luke helps us understand that the desolation is connected to Jerusalem being surrounded by armies.

   But when you see Jerusalem surrounded by armies, then know that its desolation has come near. Then let those who are in Judea flee to the mountains, and let those who are inside the city depart, and let not those who are out in the country enter it, for these are days of vengeance, to fulfill all that is written (Luke 21:20-22).

   We know from historians like Flavius Josephus that the temple was desecrated by infighting Jewish sects and the Roman army.

4. The tribulation described here was the result of the Roman army, which had gathered in the Jezreel Valley (Armageddon), laying seize to Jerusalem from 67 A.D. to 70 A.D. The condi-

tions in Jerusalem were indescribably awful according to Josephus. They ate their own children and threw dead bodies over the wall in mass. It truly was a tribulation like no other.

5. Jesus comes on the clouds. His return this time is in judgment on the generation that has rejected full and final revelation.

   So that on you may come all the righteous blood shed on earth, from the blood of innocent Abel to the blood of Zechariah the son of Barachiah, whom you murdered between the sanctuary and the altar. Truly, I say to you, all these things will come upon this generation (Matthew 23:35-36).

   For these are days of vengeance, to fulfill all that is written (Luke 21:22).

   "Coming on clouds" is a common expression of God's activity, especially in judgment (see Is. 19:1; Jer. 4:13; Ezek. 30:3; Ps. 18:9-12; 104:3; Joel 2:1-2; Zeph. 1:14-15). Jesus is using judgment language that would be familiar with those who had a knowledge of the Old Testament Scriptures. Likewise using heavenly bodies like sun, moon, and stars to depict conflict and judgment was common among prophetic language (see Is. 13:10, 24:23; Ezek. 32:7; Joel 2:10, 3:15; Amos 5:20; Zeph. 1:15; Acts 2:20).

6. The lesson of the fig tree (and all the trees; see Lk. 21:29) is that when you see the leaf begin to sprout, you know that summer is near. Likewise when you see the armies surrounding Jerusalem, the time has come to leave the city. Judgment on God's enemies is at hand. The enemies were those of His own people (see Jn. 1:11).

Some have made an issue of the fig tree being the establishment of Israel as a nation in 1948. There is nothing in Scripture to support such speculation. God judged natural Israel and released His people from identification with the unbelieving generation. The climactic judgment on Jerusalem in 70 A.D. was a redemption and release for the new creation—the Church made up of believers, both Jews and gentiles.

7. "This generation will not pass away." Some have tried to interpret this as referring to some generation in the future which sees these signs. This is a major hermeneutical leap in exegesis. It is a case of making the Scripture fit one's scheme. Jesus answered the question asked by His disciples. In that generation, the temple was destroyed, the end of the Old Testament age came, judgment came through the agency of the Roman army in destruction of His enemies, and the power of the new creation gospel was released to begin the harvest.

Glossary

Apocalyptic Literature: A type of literature that communicates through symbols and uses dreams and visions as key components.

Armageddon: An area located north of Jerusalem in the Jezreel Valley. It is the gathering place for the armies who would come against Jerusalem (see Rev. 16:16). It has become symbolic of the last and biggest battle on earth.

Eschatology: The study of last things...the end...the goal of history.

Gnostics: An early heretical group who believed among other things that God is pure goodness and material is evil.

Hermeneutics: The science of interpretation.

Kerygma: The basics, as referring to the gospel; it is the core and substance of the big story of God; the essential elements.

Meta-narrative: The over arching story of history that explains the meaning of existence. All the events of time fit into this story.

Millennium: Thousand years. Mentioned once in Scripture—Revelation 20:1-6. Refers to a literal or symbolic reign of Jesus on earth.

Prophecy clock: A term used by some to refer to the measurement of time related to the "70 weeks" prophesied by Daniel. The dispensational view supposes a gap of time between the 69th week and the final week. In that scheme the key to interpreting the future is discovering the event that starts the final week (of years). That event would start the prophecy clock.

Pre-millennial Dispensationalism: The school of thought that promotes two separate people of God: Israel and Church, with two separate plans. It includes the secret rapture of the Church which inaugurates seven years of tribulation on earth. The Jews return to Palestine where two-thirds will be slaughtered in the battle of Armageddon. Finally, God's rule will be centered in Jerusalem and the restored temple will be the focus of the earth's worship.

Presupposition: A perspective we hold unconsciously that interprets the world to us.

Replacement Theology: A phrase used by proponents of dispensational theology to define those who would not agree that God has two separate peoples: Israel and Church.

Transcendent: Greater than time and space.

Zionism: An international movement originally for the establishment of a Jewish national or religious community in Palestine under the support of modern Israel.

Annotated Bibliography

The books contained in this list were helpful to me as I researched the eschatological issues in preparing to write this book. I think they will be helpful to you in rethinking eschatological issues from a biblical perspective. I do not necessarily endorse any of these books in their entirety; however, I do not hesitate to recommend them for stimulation of thought.

Abanes, Richard. *End Time Visions.* (Nashville, TN: Broadman & Holman Publishers) 1999. **This book is an excellent overview of eschatological issues.**

Caringola, Robert. *Seventy Weeks: The Historical Alternative.* (Springfield, MO: Abundant Life Reformed Press) 1991. **Caringola offers an alternative interpretation of Daniel's seventy weeks of history.**

Crenshaw, Curtis and Grover Dunn. *Dispensationalism Today, Yesterday and Tomorrow.* (Memphis, TN: Footstool Publications) 1994. **The title fully describes this book. It presents a historical survey of dispensationalism.**

DeMar, Gary. *Last Days Madness.* (Powder Springs, GA: American Vision) 1999. **DeMar's book offers a helpful confrontation of the fascination with end-time prophecy.**

Dumbrell, William. *The Search for Order: Biblical Eschatology in Focus.* (Grand Rapids, MI: Baker Book House) 1994. **Dumbrell offers an excellent panoramic view of the different positions of eschatology.**

Gentry, Kenneth Jr. *The Beast of Revelation.* (Powder Springs, GA: American Vision) 2002. **Gentry holds to an early date for the writing of the Revelation and demonstrates how that effects interpretation. A good and thought-provoking work even if you disagree with his date.**

Goldsworthy, Graeme. *The Goldsworthy Trilogy.* (Carlisle, UK: Paternoster Press) 2000. **Goldsworthy presents an excellent study of the Kingdom of God as the central theme of Salvation history.**

Greenslade, Philip. *A Passion for God's Story: Discovering Your Place in God's Strategic Plan.* (Carlisle, UK: Paternoster Press) 2003. **This book is a must read for those desiring to see the continuity of the Old and New Testaments.**

Ice, Thomas and Kenneth L. Gentry, Jr. *The Great Tribulation Past or Future?* (Grand Rapids, MI: Kregel Publications) 1999. **This book is a debate between the two extreme views of eschatology: dispensational and preterist. Ice, the dispensationalist, and Gentry, the preterist, argue their sides effectively and focus on some points that need to be clarified.**

Kik, J. Marcellus. *An Eschatology of Victory.* (Philipsburg, NJ: P & R Publishing) 1992. **Kik offers a valuable contribution to the discussion.**

Kyle, Richard. *The Last Days Are Here Again.* (Grand Rapids, MI: Baker Book House) 1998. **The title of this book is one of my favorites—satirizing the prophecies of the end throughout history. Kyle presents a good overview of** *the times and events in history that give rise to the expectations of the end.*

LaRondelle, Hans K. *The Israel of God in Prophecy.* (Berrien Springs, MI: Andrews University Press) 1983. **This book is a study in the various, but essential, elements of prophetic interpretation.**

Mauro, Philip. *The Hope of Israel.* (Sterling, VA: Grace Abounding Ministries) 1988. **Mauro confronts the identity of Israel, and offers some thought-provoking challenges to the restoration of natural Israel.**

Murray, Iain H. *Puritan Hope.* (Edinburgh, UK: Banner of Truth Trust) 1975. **Murray presents some good, thought-provoking ideas from established thinkers of the past. This book is especially helpful in evaluating modern "pop" theology.**

Robertson, O. Palmer. *The Israel of God: Yesterday, Today, and Tomorrow.* (Phillipsburg, NJ: P & R Publishing) 2000. **This is an excellent and thought-provoking book.**

Sproul, R.C. *The Last Days According to Jesus.* (Grand Rapids, MI: Baker Book House) 2000. **R.C. Sproul is a popular modern theologian who reexamines the preterist view of eschatology and raises some interesting and important questions. Sproul offers an excellent survey of the spectrum of ideas on the preterist side of the debate.**

Witherington III, Ben. *The Paul Quest.* (Downers Grove, IL: Intervarsity Press) 2001. **It is essential that we understand Paul's theology if we are to grasp the New Testament. Witherington is a great help in putting the pieces together and presenting a comprehensive look of Pauline theology.**

Wright, Christopher J. H. *Knowing Jesus Through the Old Testament.* (Downers Grove, IL: InterVarsity Press) 1995. **Chris Wright's book is a great read and an excellent help in understanding the whole story of the Bible. He shows how Jesus is the theme of the entire Bible, not just the New Testament.**

Wright, N. T. *The Climax of the Covenant: Christ and the Law in Pauline Theology.* (Minneapolis, MN: Fortress Press) 1994. **Wright presents one of the best concepts of covenant and the continuity of the Old and New Testaments. I definitely recommend that you read this one.**

Dudley Hall is president of Successful Christian Living Ministries. For 30 years, Successful Christian Living Ministries has been effective in helping thousands of people implement the life transforming truths of God's Word into their practical daily living. Through seminars, retreats, conferences, and special events, as well as books, audio & video materials, and training courses, SCLM has emphasized the availability of God's abundant grace, the simplicity of life in His plan, and the hope offered through His powerful promises.

"Believing that true success is achieved only by alignment with God's design, SCLM is committed to helping the individual, the family, and the Church find and fulfill that design."

For more information on Dudley, his Monthly Message Tape/CD subscription, his weekly devotional subscriptions, or any of the various ministry opportunities offered by SCLM, please contact us at:

SUCCESSFUL CHRISTIAN LIVING MINISTRIES

P.O. Box 101
Euless, Texas 76039

817-267-9224
www.sclm.org

Additional copies of this book and other
book titles from DESTINY IMAGE are
available at your local bookstore.

For a bookstore near you, call 1-800-722-6774.

Send a request for a catalog to:

Destiny Image₍ᵣ₎ Publishers, Inc.
P.O. Box 310
Shippensburg, PA 17257-0310

*"Speaking to the Purposes of God for This
Generation and for the Generations to Come"*

For a complete list of our titles,
visit us at www.destinyimage.com